CW00569963

'The late Bill Hicks once famously pleaded with advertisers and marketers to kill themselves. "You are Satan's spawn, filling the world with bile and garbage, you are fucked and you are fucking us, kill yourselves, it's the only way to save your fucking soul. Kill yourself, kill yourself, kill yourself now." This novel feels like a 259-page elaboration of this idea: passion and expletives included. And most of it is excellent . . . A must-read, tell-all-your-friends book . . . Brilliant'
Scarlett Thomas, *Independent on Sunday*

'Those who make a living in advertising are seldom allowed to grow old gracefully. Beigbeder (ex-Young & Rubicam, something of a lit celeb in his native France) is no exception: he was fired from his job for writing this expose of the industry. £6.99 recounts the story of a disillusioned ad exec who turns to violence to vent his rage on the consuming public and those who manipulate us. Frenetic, funny and bleak'
Marie Claire

'This isn't throwaway self-deprecation with the occasional undertow of violence, but talk of ideas'
Omer Ali, *Time Out*

'Octave is an advertising executive, 33, overpaid, coked up, nihilistic and contemptuous of his job. He wants to be sacked so he can collect his unemployment insurance, but the worse he behaves, the more successful he becomes. Meanwhile, he writes this furious condemnation of the entire business of advertising and consumption . . . Octave delivers plenty of boiling denunciations of what life is like in a big advertising company and of how consumers are manipulated'
David Sexton, *Evening Standard*

'Full of sex and romance, cynicism and philosophy'
Lorna Russell, *Big Issue*

'One minute you're immersed in the denigration of capitalism, the next the protagonists start messily killing each other. Two books in one. Both of them good'
FHM

Frédéric Beigbeder is the author of three novels, *Mémoires d'un jeune homme dérangé*, *Vacances dans le coma* and *L'Amour dure trois ans*, and a collection of short stories, *Nouvelles sous ecstasy*. He is also a literary critic for TV, radio and magazine. While writing this novel he was on the staff of an advertising agency (Young & Rubicam). When you've finished £6.99 you'll know why he isn't any longer.

Adriana Hunter has been a freelance translator and writer since 1989. She has translated more than twelve books, including two novels by Agnès Desarthe, Sophie Marceau's experimental first novel *Telling Lies*, and Catherine Millet's explicit autobiography, *The Sexual life of Catherine M*. She lives in Norfolk with her husband and their three children.

a novel

Translated from the French
by Adriana Hunter

Picador

First published 2002 by Picador

This edition published 2014 by Picador
an imprint of Pan Macmillan, a division of Macmillan Publishers Limited
Pan Macmillan, 20 New Wharf Road, London N1 9RR
Basingstoke and Oxford
Associated companies throughout the world
www.panmacmillan.com

ISBN 978-1-4472-7222-9

Translation copyright © Macmillan Publishers Ltd 2002
Copyright © Frédéric Beigbeder 2002

The right of Frédéric Beigbeder to be identified as the
author of this work and of Adriana Hunter as the translator
has been asserted by them in accordance with the
Copyright, Designs and Patents Act 1988.

Originally published 2000 in a slightly different version as
99 francs by Editions Grasset & Fasquelle, Paris

The Macmillan Group has no responsibility for the information
provided by and author websites whose address you obtain from
this book ('author websites'). The inclusion of author website
addresses in this book does not constitute an endorsement by or
association with us of such sites or the content, products,
advertising or other materials presented on such sites.

A CIP catalogue record for this book is available from
the British Library.

Phototypeset by Intype london Ltd

Bruno Le Moult is no more.
That's who this book was for.

Given that that's the score,

It's for you Chloë dear,
You've only just got here.

'There is, of course, no reason why the new totalitarianisms should resemble the old. Government by clubs and firing squads, by artificial famine, mass imprisonment and mass deportation, is not merely inhumane (nobody cares much about that nowadays); it is demonstrably inefficient – and in an age of advanced technology, inefficiency is the sin against the Holy Ghost. A really efficient totalitarian state would be one in which the all-powerful executive of political bosses and their army of managers control a population of slaves who do not have to be coerced, because they love their servitude. To make them love it is the task assigned, in present-day totalitarian states, to ministries of propaganda, newspaper editors and school-teachers'
Aldous Huxley, introduction to *Brave New World*, 1946

'We are afflicted
By the desires they have inflicted upon us'
Alain Souchon, *Foule sentimentale*, 1993

'Capitalism has survived communism.
Now it only remains for it to consume itself'
Charles Bukowski, *Le capitaine est parti déjeuner et les marins se sont emparés du bateau*, 1998.

£6.99 is a translation from Frédéric Beigbeder's *99 francs*. The setting of the novel has also been transposed – from Paris to London – and so the English edition differs in some respects from the original.

The names have been changed
to protect the guilty

1 I

'What we cannot change,
we should at least describe.'

Rainer Werner Fassbinder

1

Everything is transient: love, art, the planet Earth, you, me. Death is so inevitable that it takes everyone by surprise. How do you know whether this day will be your last? You always think you've got time. And then suddenly, that's it, you go and drown, your allotted time is up. Death is the only meeting that hasn't been keyed into your personal organizer.

Everything can be bought: love, art, the planet Earth, you, me. I'm writing this book to get myself fired. If I handed in my notice, I wouldn't be able to claim benefit. I have to cut the branch from underneath myself. My freedom goes by the name of unemployment insurance. I'd rather be fired by a firm than by life itself. BECAUSE I'M FRIGHTENED. My colleagues are falling like flies around me: a drowning in a swimming pool, a cocaine overdose dressed up as a heart attack, a crash in a private jet, a spin in a convertible that spun out of control. Then last night I dreamed that I was drowning. I saw myself sinking through the water, brushing past manta rays with my lungs full of water. There was a pretty woman on the beach in the distance, calling me. I didn't call back to her because my mouth was full of salt water. I was drowning but I couldn't call for help. And everyone in the sea with me was doing the same thing. They were all sinking without calling for help. I think it's time I left everything behind, because I've forgotten how to float.

Everything is transient and everything can be bought. Man is a product like any other, with a sell-by date. That's why I've decided to retire at thirty-three. Apparently it's the optimum age for resuscitations.

2

My name is Octave and I'm dressed from head to foot in Tom Ford. I'm an advertising executive: Yup, that's right, I pollute the universe. I'm the guy who sells you shit. Who makes you dream of things you'll never have. The sky's always blue, the girls are never ugly, perfect happiness touched up on Photoshop. Immaculate images, in-yer-face music. When, after painstaking saving, you manage to buy the car of your dreams (the one I shot in my last campaign), I will already have made it look out of date. I'm three trends ahead, and I make sure you're always frustrated. Glamour is a country that no one ever gets to. I intoxicate you with new things, and the advantage with the new is that it never stays new for long. There are always new new things to make the last lot look old. I want to make you drool – that's my vocation. No one in my profession actually wants you to be happy, because happy people don't spend.

Your suffering boosts sales. In our own jargon we call this the 'post-purchase downer'. There's some product that you just have to have, but as soon as you've got it there's something else you have to have. Hedonism isn't a humanism; it's cash-flow. What does it say? 'I spend, therefore I am.' But in order to create a need I have to arouse jealousy, pain and dissatisfaction: they are my weapons. And my target – is you.

I spend my life lying to you, and I'm paid a shed-load for it. I earn around £12k a month (excluding the expenses, the company car, the stock options and the golden parachute). I should say 19,440 euros really, because I would look richer. Still, do you know many guys earning this much at my age? I manipulate you and they give me the new Mercedes SLK (the one with the roof which slides automatically into the boot) or the BMW Z8 or the Porsche Boxster or the Mazda MX5. (Personally, I'm a sucker for the BMW Z8 roadster: the aerodynamic aesthetics of its bodywork combined with the grace and power of its straight six-cylinder engine producing 400 b.h.p. and giving a 0 to 60 time of 5.4 seconds. Better still, the thing looks like a giant suppository, just right for giving the world one up the arse.)

I interrupt your films on TV to bombard you with my logos, and they give me a holiday in St Barths or Phuket or St Moritz. I bang on and on at you with my slogans in your favourite magazines, and they offer me a château in the Périgord or a manor house in Gloucestershire or a villa in Tuscany or a condo in Aspen or a palace in Morocco or a catamaran in the Caribbean or a yacht in St Tropez. I'm everywhere. You'll never get away from me. Wherever you look, you'll find one of my ads centre-stage. I forbid you to be bored. I stop you thinking. The terrorist cult of the new helps me to sell empty space. Ask any surfer: to stay on the surface you have to have a gap, a pocket of air, underneath you. Surfing is just sliding over an abyss (whiz kids on the

Internet know that as well as the Malibu champions). I decree what is True, what is Beautiful and what is Good. I cast the models who'll be giving you a hard-on in six months' time. I plaster their images in so many places that you call them super-models; these young girls of mine will traumatize every woman over fourteen. You idolize my choices. This winter, you've got to have breasts up above your shoulders and a seriously underpopulated pussy. The more I play with your subconscious, the more you obey me. If I sing the praises of a new yoghurt on the walls of your town, I can guarantee that you're going to buy it. You think you've got your own free will, but sooner or later you'll recognize my product on a supermarket shelf and you'll buy it, just like that, just to taste it. Believe me. I know my job.

Ohh, it feels so good when I get inside your head. Oh yes, yes, I'm coming inside your right hemisphere. What you want is no longer yours to choose: I'll tell you what you want. I won't let you want just anything, though. What you think you want is the result of an investment that runs into millions of pounds. I decide today what you'll be wanting tomorrow.

Probably none of this makes me seem very sympathetic in your eyes. Usually when you start writing a book, you try to be likeable and all that, but I don't want to hide the truth: I'm not going to be a nice narrator. In fact I'm really one of the bad guys who destroys everything he touches. Ideally, you'll hate *me* straight away and then the social climate that created me.

Don't you think it's amazing how normal everyone

thinks this situation is? You disgust me, you pathetic little slaves, subject to my every whim. Why have you let me become King of the World? I'd like to get to the bottom of this mystery. How is it that, at the very height of an age of cynicism, advertising was crowned Emperor? It's about 2,000 years since a cretin like me has had so much power.

I'd like to leave everything behind, to get out of here with my haul, taking some drugs and some whores off to some crappy little desert island. (I could watch Soraya and Tamara fingering each other all day while I polished my rocket.) But I haven't got the balls to hand in my notice. That's why I'm writing this book. Getting fired would get me out of this gilded cage. I could do you damage, so stop me before it's too late, please! Just give us a hundred thou' and I'll scarper, Scout's honour. So people have replaced God with consumer goods, what do you want me to do about it?

I'm smiling because what if, as soon as this book is published, I'm not kicked out but given a promotion? In the world that I'm going to describe to you, they stomach criticism, they encourage insolence, they pay you to inform on others and they make use of your diatribes. Soon they'll be awarding a Nobel Prize for Provocation and I'll be the candidate no one else can beat. Rebellion is all part of the game. In the past, dictatorships were afraid of freedom of expression, they censored every challenge, locked up all the writers, burned controversial books. In the good old days of evil Inquisitions and burnings at the stake you could tell the goodies from the baddies. The totalitarianism of advertising is far cleverer at washing its hands. This particular brand of fascism has learned from the mistakes of its predecessors (Berlin 1945 and Berlin 1989 – why is it that barbarities like these all came to an end in the same city?).

Advertising has chosen a low profile, the soft touch, the art of persuasion, to reduce humanity to slavery. We're living in the first system in which man is dominated by something against which even the concept of freedom is utterly powerless. Quite the opposite, in fact, it's banking on freedom, freedom is its greatest find. Every critique shows freedom in a good light, every pamphlet reinforces the illusion of its gentle tolerance. It subjugates you so elegantly. Everything is permitted, no one's going to come and give you a hard time if you do a runner. The system has achieved its goal: even disobedience has become a form of obedience.

Our shattered future is so nicely presented on the printed page. And as you're reading this book I'm sure that you're actually saying, 'Ah, he's rather sweet, this little ad man, biting the hand that feeds him. Come on now, get back in your box. You're stuck just like the rest of us, you'll pay your taxes like everyone else.' There's no way out. Everything is locked up, with a bright smile on its face. Your route is barred by repayments, monthly instalments and interest. Go ahead, have your nervous breakdown – there are millions of unemployed out there just waiting for you to vacate the space. You can whinge as much as you like, Churchill's already given you the reply. He said, 'Democracy is the worst form of government except all the other forms.' He was no traitor. He didn't say it was the best system; he said it was the *worst*.

3

At nine o'clock this morning I breakfasted with the director of marketing from the Dairy Products department at Damione International, one of the biggest food-processing companies in the world (£8,500 billion turnover in 2000). We met in their bunker of steel and glass decorated *à la* Albert Speer. You have to show your credentials just to get into the place: the yoghurt empire is a high-security area. Never have dairy products been so well protected. All that's missing is the best-before date over the automatic doors. They gave me a card with a magnetic strip to gain access to the lifts, then I went through the metal barriers (like the ones in tube stations), between a pair of double doors, and I suddenly felt mega-important, as if I had a meeting with the queen, for goodness' sake, when I was actually just going to see some guy in a stripy shirt who'd done quite well in business school.

In the lift a verse from Michel Houellebecq came back to me:

> Employees rising up towards their Calvary
> In elevators like shiny nickel ships
> I notice every passing secretary
> Touching up the gloss on her lips.

And it felt very strange being a part of such a cold poem.

Come to think of it, this morning's meeting probably really was more important than an interview with the head of state. It was the most important meeting of my life, because it decided the rest of my life.

On the eighth floor at Damione all the product managers wear stripy shirts and ties with little animals on them. The director of marketing terrorizes his fat personal assistants, who get fluid retention problems from the stress. His name is Alfred Dewler. Dewler begins all his meetings with the same words: 'We're not here for our own pleasure, but for the consumer's pleasure.' As if the consumer were from a completely different race – an 'Untermensch'? He makes me want to puke, and for someone who works in the food industry, that's a problem. I imagine him in the mornings shaving, tying his tie, traumatizing his children with his bad breath, listening to twenty-four-hour news on the radio far too loud, reading the *FT* as he stands in the kitchen downing his coffee. He hasn't touched his wife since 1975, but he doesn't even cheat on her (she does on him, though). He reads only one book a year and it's written by Fay Weldon. He puts on his suit. He sincerely believes that he plays an important role within his holding company. He has a great fat Mercedes which goes vroom-vroom when he's stuck in the traffic and a Motorola which goes pilim-pilim in its little case just above the Pioneer car radio that broadcasts messages for Peugeot – the drive of your life, Tesco – every little helps, Sanatogen – for life's little ups and downs. He's convinced that the rise in inflation is good news, whereas all inflation really represents is more and more useless products, 'a massive accumulation of merchandise' (Karl Marx), a mountain of supplementary objects to bury us. He has Faith. He learned that at his smart business school: Thou shalt have Faith in Inflation. Let us produce millions of tons of products and we shall all find happiness! Glory be to expansion which makes the factories hum, which makes expansion grow! But, above all, never stop to think!

We're sitting in a drab meeting room just like meeting rooms in every office block all over the world, round a big oval table with glasses of orange juice on it, stifling in the sweaty armpit smell left from the late meeting yesterday. A secretary-slave brings in a pot of coffee and never looks up.

Dewler starts the meeting by making it clear that 'Everything we say here is strictly confidential. There will be no minutes for this meeting. This is a crisis meeting. We'll have to look at the sales figures but I'm worried about turnover. One of our competitors is launching a me-too product with a big campaign. Various sources agree that they want to steal some of our market share. We see this as an attack.' In a fraction of a second, every person round the table starts nodding and frowning. All they need are the khaki hats and the maps on the table and they could be in *The Longest Day*.

After the usual meteorological comments, Jeffrey, our agency's commercial director, addresses the meeting and gives them an outline of the brief, using powerpoint to illustrate what he's saying.

'So, we've just shown you a thirty-second script to defend Yoplite against this attack from the me-too distri-

butors. I'd like to remind you all of the strategic objective
we set ourselves at the last meeting. "In a shrinking market,
Yoplite is innovative and intends to give fromage frais a
new image and vision with its new ergonomic packaging." '

He looks up from his papers and changes the trans-
parency. These words appear on the wall in bold type:

Subliminal points to get across (cont.):
Emotional

               Delicious/irresistible

Pleasure/Fashion   **YOPLITE**   **Slimming/Beauty**

Healthy/Nutritious

                      Rational

They all seem to be taking this sitting down, so he just
carries on paraphrasing the text that his assistant (whose
child was busy going down with an ear infection in the
local day nursery) typed out for him in Word 6.

'As we agreed with Luke and Alfred on the 23rd, our
ideas emphasize the benefits for the consumer: "With
Yoplite, I stay slim but I'm also eating something that's
good for me because of the vitamins and the calcium
content." In what is a highly competitive sector, the brand
review highlighted the fact that we have to put across this
double insight: beauty plus health. Yoplite is good for my
body and my mind. You win all round, top and . . . bottom.
Ha ha hem.'

This speech is the product of much reflection in the
Strategic Planning department (two depressive quad-
ragenarians) and from Jeff's two assistant-directors of

advertising (fresh from their Media Studies course in Manchester). It hinges principally on what the customer wants and likes, and – more importantly – justifies the script I hatched last night. At this point Jeff stops laughing because he feels a bit out on a limb. He goes on with his contortions:

'We've come up with a federative concept which, while adhering to the original strategy, will, I believe, allow us to confer maximum impact on the product promise, especially on a visual level. Right, well, over to Octave.'

Given that I'm Octave, it's clearly time to break the deathly silence and talk them through the idea for the thirty-second sequence, showing them the storyboard of twelve colour pictures sketched by an overpaid draughtsman.

'Right then, we're on Malibu beach in California. It's a fantastic day. Two beautiful blondes are running along the beach in red swimming costumes. Suddenly one of them says, "Onomastic exegesis is threatened by prohibitive hermeneutics." The other replies, "Don't let yourself slip into ontological paronomase." Meanwhile, two tanned surfers are arguing in the water. The first says, "Don't you realize Nietzsche's *Ecce Homo* is a completely hedonistic eulogy to swimming?" The other replies angrily, "No, no, he's just defending the concept of 'Great good health' as an allegorical solipsism!" We come back to the beach, where the girls are now writing mathematical equations in the sand. Dialogue: "If we work on the hypothesis that the cube root of x varies in direct relation with infinity . . ." "Yes," says the other, "then you just have to subdivide the total to obtain an asymptotic solution." '

'The sequence ends with a shot of the Yoplite pot with the baseline: "YOPLITE. BEING SLIM is GOOD FOR YOUR BRAIN."'

The silence continues to feel silent. The director of marketing looks at his product managers; they're taking notes to avoid having an opinion. Jeffrey tries rather unconvincingly to brighten the atmosphere with a tap-dancer's flourish, then resumes.

'Obviously there's the "mm Damione" signature at the end, that goes without saying. Um . . . we thought it would be interesting to take symbols of "slim" and "beautiful" and to show them having very intellectual conversations . . . You also have to realize that outdoor sports are becoming increasingly mainstream. And, well, there would be possible variations: Miss World contestants arguing about geo-politics, especially the 1918 Treaty of Brest-Litovsk; Chippendales in the buff discussing nudity as corporeal freedom of expression and as a negation of postmodern alienation, not without showing off their muscles, etc. Fun idea, isn't it?'

The various assistant-directors take it in turn to give their comment: 'I quite like it', 'I'm pretty much for it', 'I'm not mega-convinced but I do get the idea', 'It's worth investigating' . . . It's also worth mentioning that, like parrots, each of them repeats exactly what his hierarchical inferior has just said. Until it's Dewler's turn to speak. The big boss doesn't agree with his subordinates.

'Why do we need humour?'

Alfred Dewler's right, actually. If I were him, I wouldn't

be laughing either. Repressing my rising need to vomit, I respond.

'It's good for your brand name. Humour makes you seem like a friend. And it's excellent for memorization. Consumers remember things that make them laugh. They tell each other the joke when they go out to dinner, at work, in the school playground. Look at the comedies that are doing well at the moment. And when people go to the cinema they like to laugh too . . .'

Alfred Dewler drops this immortal sentence: 'Yes, but they don't eat the film afterwards.'

I ask to be excused to go to the toilet, thinking, 'You – you great shit – you've earned your place in my book. You'll have your rightful part in it. No later than chapter 3. ALFRED DEWLER IS A BIG SHIT.'

All writers are tell-tales, sneaks. All writing is a denunciation, a betrayal. I can't see the point in writing a book if it's not to spill the beans. It so happens that I've seen some things in my time and, incidentally, I know an editor mad enough to let me tell my story. I didn't ask for anything in the beginning. I found myself right in the middle of a machine which was devastating everything in its path. I never pretended that I would come out of it unscathed. I looked everywhere for someone who had the power to change the world, until the day I realized that it could be me.

4

Broadly speaking, their idea was to tear down the forests and replace them with cars. It wasn't a conscious, considered plan; it was far worse than that. They had no idea where they were heading, but they went there all the same, whistling on their way – and after them came the flood, the downpour (or, rather, the acid rain). For the first time in the history of the planet, humans from every country had the same goal: earning enough money to live like an advertisement. Everything else was incidental, they wouldn't be there to suffer the consequences.

One little point needs clarifying. I'm not having a go at myself here, nor doing a bit of public psychoanalysis. I'm writing the confessions of a child of the millennium. If I use the term 'confession', it is in the Catholic sense of the word. I want to save my soul before I get out of here. I must remind you that 'there is more joy in heaven and earth over one sinner who repents than over ninety-nine just persons which need no repentance' (Gospel according to St Luke). From now on the only person with whom I will agree to enter into an open-ended contract is God.

I would like you to bear in mind that I tried to resist, even if I knew that being present at those meetings was in itself a collaboration. Just by sitting at their table, in their morbid, marbled, air-conditioned rooms, you're participating in the general brainwashing. Their hawkish vocabulary gives them away: they talk of *campaigns, targets, strategies, impact.* They plan *objectives*, a *first wave*, a *second wave.* They're afraid of being *cannibalized*, and refuse to have the *lifeblood* sucked out of them. Apparently in the Mars Group (a chocolate-bar manufacturers named after the God of War), they count the year in thirteen periods of four weeks; they don't say 1 April but 'P4 W1'! They're well and truly soldiers carrying out the Third World War. I will remind you, if I may, that if advertising is a technique of cerebral intoxication invented by the American Albert Davis Lasker in 1899, it was certainly very efficiently developed by one Joseph Goebbels during the 1930s, with the intention of convincing the German people to burn all the Jews. Goebbels was a highly skilled advertising copywriter: 'DEUTSCHLAND ÜBER ALLES', 'EIN VOLK, EIN REICH, EIN FÜHRER', 'ARBEIT MACHT FREI' . . . If there's much ado about advertising, it's probably with good cause.

To consume can also mean to burn.

At one time I thought that I might be the grain of sand in the machine. The rebel inside the beast's still-fertile belly; a first-class soldier in the infantry of the global marketplace. I used to say, 'You can't divert an aeroplane without getting inside it, you have to change things from the inside, as Gramsci said.' (Gramsci sounds more chic than Trotsky but he still advocates the same entryism. I could just as easily have cited Tony Blair or Lionel Jospin.) It helped me do my dirty work. In Paris the rebels of '68 started out with a revolution then went into advertising – I just wanted to go the other way.

I saw myself as a sort of liberal Che Guevara, a revolutionary in a Gucci jacket. That's it, I was Captain Gucche! Viva el Gucche! What a great brand name. So easy to remember. Two problems with the concept:

1) It sounds like 'Duce'.
2) The greatest revolutionary of the twentieth century wasn't Che Guevara but Mikhail Gorbachev.

When I went home to my enormous flat in the evenings, I would sometimes have trouble sleeping, thinking about the homeless. Actually, it was the coke that kept me awake. That metallic taste stuck in my throat. I'd have a wank in the basin before taking a sleeping pill. I'd get up at about midday. I didn't have a wife any longer.

I think that fundamentally I wanted to do good and create happiness around me. That wasn't possible for two reasons: because people stopped me and because I abdicated. It's always the people motivated by the best of intentions who turn into monsters. Now I know that will change, it would be impossible, it's too late. You can't fight an adversary who is all around you, is virtual and knows no pain. Contrary to the views of Pierre de Coubertin, I would say that the most important thing nowadays is *not* to participate. You have to get out, like Gauguin, John Cleese or Castenada, that's all there is to it. Heading off to a desert island where Angelica spreads tanning lotion on to Juliana's breasts while Juliana gives you a hand-job. Tending your garden . . . of marijuana, and just hoping you'll be dead before the end of the world. The brand names have won the Third World War against the humans. The strange thing about the Third World War is that all the countries lost it at the same time. I can give you a scoop: David never slays Goliath. I was naïve. Candour is not a desirable characteristic in this corporation. I've been had over a barrel. Which, interestingly enough, is the only thing I have in common with you.

5

I puked up my twelve cups of coffee in the toilets of Damione International, then I did a quick line to set myself up again. I splashed my face with ice-cold water and went back to the meeting. It's hardly surprising that there aren't any creative designers who want to work for Damione. They really milk you there. But I had more ideas up my sleeve: I suggested a pastiche of *Charlie's Angels* with three pretty girls prancing around with pistols trained on the camera set to 1970s soul music. They stop criminals and wrong-doers by reciting Keats to them (backed up by judo holds, kung-fu kicks, somersaults and other gymnastics); then one of them looks into the camera as she twists the arm of some unfortunate gangster groaning in pain and cries, 'We wouldn't have been able to carry out this arrest without Fruit Yoplite 0% fat. When you need to be in shape – mind and body!'

This suggestion was no more garlanded with success than any of the following: a parody of a structuralist Hindu film, James Bond girls talking to their shrinks, a Peter Greenaway remake of *Wonderwoman*, a Julia Kristeva conference shot by David Hamilton . . .

The global village idiot went on with his diatribe against humour.

'You creative designers, you really think you're artists. All you can think about is winning prizes at Cannes, but I'm accountable for this. I'm in a Go/No Go situation with this. We've got stock to shift on the shelves. We *have* to, do you understand? Octave, I like you very much, your jokes make me laugh, but I'm not a housewife in her forties. We're working to a specific market, we have to put our own susceptibilities aside and adapt to our target, to think about how the displays are going to look in Iceland . . .'

'You mean like the northern lights?' I cut in chirpily.

The man from Damione didn't laugh. He launched into a description of how the trials had gone. His underlings carried on scribbling on their notepads.

'We got twelve shoppers together and they didn't get anything out of your flights of fancy. They couldn't tell us anything about the product afterwards. What they want is information, to be shown the product and the price, end of story. And, anyway, where's my key visual in all this? Your creative ideas are all very well but I've come to this from manufacturing detergents and I need something that I can adapt to use in the supermarkets. And how am I supposed to do my Internet advertising? The Americans are already busy "spamming" customers with e-mail promotions and your thinking is still somewhere in the twentieth century. You're not going to do this to me. I've learned the hard way with detergents. The only thing that counts is market share. So, I'm happy to go along with an amazing new idea, but it's got to respect the various constraints.'

I made a huge effort to remain calm.

'Mr Dewler, could I ask you a question? How do you intend to amaze your consumers if you ask them for their opinion first? Would you, for example, ask your wife to choose the surprise you want to give her for her next birthday?'

'My wife hates surprises.'

'Is that why she married you?'

Jeffrey was overcome by a fit of coughing.

However politely I smiled at Dewler, I couldn't help thinking of Adolf Hitler's words: 'If you want the masses to like you, you should tell them only the simplest and most obvious things.' Such contempt, such hatred for the people, perceiving them as a sort of vague entity . . . I sometimes feel that these industrialists would almost be prepared to get the cattle trucks out again if it would make the public eat their products. Could I risk three more quotations? 'We're not looking for the truth, just the effect on the people.' 'Propaganda ceases to work as soon as its presence becomes apparent.' 'The bigger the lie, the easier it is to believe.' Those are from Joseph Goebbels (him again).

Alfred Dewler went on with his diatribe.

'Our target is to shift 12,000 tonnes this year. Your girls running along the beach talking about philosophy are too intellectual. That's fine among the media darlings at the Groucho Club, but the average consumer's going to get sod all out of it! As for mentioning *Ecce Homo*, I know what you're talking about but the general public . . . they might think it's some gay thing! No, frankly, you're going to have to rework this whole concept. I'm really sorry. You know, at Damione we have a dictum: "Don't think people are stupid, but never forget that they are." '

'But that's terrible! That implies that democracy leads to self-destruction. It's maxims like that that'll bring back fascism. You start by saying that people are stupid, then you just do away with them.'

'Oh, come on! You're not going to do a star turn as the revolutionary artist. We're selling yoghurt here, we're not about to start a revolution. What's the matter with him today? Didn't they let you into Spearmint Rhino last night or something?'

The atmosphere was getting uncomfortable. Jeffrey tried to divert the conversation:

'But to be honest the discrepancy between these sexy girls and their conversation about hermeneutics. . . . it says exactly what you want to say: beauty and intellect . . . Am I right?'

'It's too many words to put along the sides of lorries. You'd slice the heads off the lorry drivers.'

'Could I remind you,' I interjected smugly, 'of one of the principles of advertising: creating a humorous effect (what we call the "creative leap") which makes the viewer smile, therefore producing a feeling of complicity, which facilitates sales of the brand? Anyway, you may well be from Damione, but your strategy is pretty half-hearted, if you don't mind my saying. "Makes you slim and intelligent", that's a hell of a unique selling proposition!'

Jeffrey made it clear that I shouldn't pursue it any further. I almost suggested we used 'DAMIONE ÜBER ALLES' as a baseline but I chickened out. You're going to think that I'm exaggerating, that it can't be as bad as all that. But look what was at stake in this morning's little meeting. It wasn't just a presentation for some everyday campaign. That meeting was more important than the Munich Agreement. (In Munich in 1938 the French and British heads of state, Edouard Daladier and Neville Chamberlain, abandoned Czechoslovakia to the Nazis, just like that, signed it off on an innocent table-top.) Hundreds of meetings like that one at Damione abandon the world every day. Thousands of daily Munichs! What's going on is crucial: ideas are being murdered, change is forbidden. These individuals have nothing but contempt for the general public. They want to keep them in a permanent, conditioned state: buying. As they see it, they're trying to get through to a 'moronic woman in her forties'. You suggest something amusing to them, something that credits the viewer with some intelligence, which tries to raise them up in some way (well, it's a matter of courtesy when you're interrupting a film on TV, isn't it?) and they won't let you. And it's always the same, every time, every day, every day . . . Thousands of 'easy options' a day, scuttling off in your Tergal suit with your tail between your legs. Thousands of easy options a day. And these hundreds of thousands of inane meetings are gradually seeing to it that calculated, contemptuous dross triumphs over the simple, naïve struggle for human progress. Ideally, in a democracy, you should want to use the extraordinary power of communication to expand people's minds, not to crush them. That never happens, because the people who wield the power don't like taking any risks. The advertisers want everything chewed over in advance and tried out in advance. They don't want to make your brain work, they want to turn you into sheep. I'm not joking, you'll see: one day they'll tattoo a bar-code on your wrist. They know that the only power you have is in your debit cards. They need to stop you choosing. They have to transform your every action into the act of buying.

Resistance to change . . . it's never more violent than in all these impersonal meeting rooms. The desire to maintain the status quo is rooted here, in this building, among these little managers with their dandruff and their natty shoes. They're entrusted with the keys to power and no one knows why. They're the centre of the universe! The politicians don't control anything any longer; the economy is governing the world. Marketing is a perverted form of democracy: the orchestra is leading the conductor. The opinion polls decide on politics, trials decide on advertising, panels choose the songs we hear on the radio, sneak previews determine how films should end, ratings govern what's on television – all those studies carried out by the Alfred Dewlers of this world. No one is responsible for anything any more, except the Alfred Dewlers. They are holding the reins, but they're not going anywhere. Big Brother is not watching you, Big Brother is testing you. But the whole ethos of opinion polls is conservative. It's a form of abdication. No one any longer has the courage to offer you something that you *might* not like. That's what's killing off innovation, originality, creativity and rebellion. Everything else follows on from there: our cloned existence . . . our blind acceptance . . . our isolation from each other . . . the anaesthetized ugliness of everything . . . No, this isn't just some little meeting. It's the beginning of the end of the world. You can't obey the world and transform it at the same time. Some day, they'll be learning in school how democracy destroyed itself.

In fifty years, they'll be pursuing Alfred Dewler for crimes against humanity. Every time that man uses the word 'market', you should take it to mean 'cake'. If he says 'market research', he means 'cake research'; 'market economics' means 'cake economics'. This man is in favour of freeing up the cake, he wants to launch new products on the cake, to commit himself to conquering new cakes, and you must never forget the fact that this is a global cake. He hates you, you should know that. As far as he's concerned, you're just cattle he wants to force-feed. You're Pavlov's dogs with your knee-jerk reactions. The only thing he's interested in is your cash in his shareholders' pockets (and they're just the American pension base, or, put another way, a load of has-beens with face-lifts busy dying beside their swimming pools in Miami). And may the best materialist world go round.

I asked Alfred Dewler to excuse me again because I could tell I was about to have a nosebleed. That's the problem with London cocaine: it's cut with so much other stuff that you have to have strong nasal passages. I could feel the blood flowing up. I got up with a huge sniff to run to the crapper, where my nose pissed blood like never before. It wouldn't stop, there was blood everywhere, on the mirror, on my shirt, on the automatic roller-towel, on the tiles, and there were great red bubbles of it coming out of my nose.

Luckily no one came in then. I looked in the mirror and saw my face covered in blood, red everywhere, on my chin, my mouth, the collar of my shirt. The basin was crimson and I had blood on my hands – this time they really had won: Quite literally *I had blood on my hands* – and it gave me an idea, so I wrote on the toilet walls 'Pigs' and 'PIGS' on the door. I went out into the corridor, pigs on the plywood, pigs on the carpet tiles, pigs in the lift, and I fled. I think the surveillance cameras must have immortalized those glorious moments. The day I baptized capitalism with my own blood.

6

Oops! The chairman of my agency has just come into my office. He's wearing white trousers, a navy-blue blazer with a white hankie in the breast pocket and gold buttons down the front, and a pink shirt, in gingham check (obviously). I only just had time to click this text off the screen. He tapped me on the shoulder paternally. 'So, working hard?' Philip likes me because he's got wind of the fact that I've kept this whole profession at arm's length. He knows that he's nothing without me – and it's reciprocal: without him, I'd have to say goodbye to the desert island, the coke and the whores (Veronica languishing on top of Fiona, who's swollen with desire while I'm inside Veronica). He's one of the people I'll miss when – along with everyone else in advertising – I get grilled once this opuscule is published. He pays me handsomely to prove his love for me. I respect him because he's got a bigger, swankier flat than me. Now he's tapping me on the shoulder oddly and whispering in a taut voice.

'Tell me . . . have you been feeling a bit tired recently?'

I shrug my shoulders.

'Ever since I was born.'

'Octave, you know we're crazy about you here. But

watch yourself. Apparently you blew a fuse this morning at Damione. Dewler rang me to yell at me, and I had to send a team of cleaners to get rid of your works of art. Perhaps you should get some rest . . .'

'Don't you think it would be better to fire me?'

Philip laughed, and patted my back again.

'Straight to big words like firing. Out of the question. We're too conscious of the talent you've got to offer. Your presence here at The Ross does us a lot of good – you know the Americans loved your film for Oranga-Cola, and your baseline "C'EST BEAUCOUP TROP WONDERFUL" scored very highly with Ipsos – but perhaps you should just go and see the client a bit less, don't you think?'

'Hang on, I kept my cool. That arsehole Dewler sermonized about "spamming" on the web. I could very easily have asked Charlie to e-mail him a Trojan Horse virus to screw up his system. That would have cost him more than a make-over in the john.'

Philip left chuckling loudly which – probably – meant that he didn't understand my jibe. What does, however, augur well for my redundancy is that the chairman came to lecture me in person, because he too could quite easily have done it by cc-mail on the Intranet. People actually talk to each other less and less; usually, when you force yourself to speak the truth to someone's face, then it's *almost* too late.

7

People often ask me why creative designers like me are so overpaid. A freelancer who takes a whole week writing an article for the *Guardian* would be paid fifty times less than a copywriter who spends ten minutes on a freelance job dreaming up a poster. Why? Quite simply because the copywriter is doing a job that brings more money in. The advertiser has an annual budget of hundreds of thousands to spend on campaigns. The agency calculates the fees as a percentage of the space price: usually a commission of 9 per cent (it used to be 15 per cent but the advertisers realized that was daylight robbery). In fact, creative designers are underpaid in relation to what they generate. When you see the money that wafts past them, the money they produce for their employers to shuffle, their salaries seem tiny in comparison. Anyway, if a copywriter asked for only a modest fee, people wouldn't take him seriously.

Once when I was coming out of a meeting with Mark Browning (my creative director) I asked him, 'Why does everyone listen to Philip and not to me?'

'Because,' he replied quick as a flash, 'he makes £30,000 a month and you don't.'

Being a copywriter isn't a job in which you have to

justify your salary; it's one where your salary justifies you. As with TV presenters, it's a very unreliable career. That's why copywriters earn in a few years what a normal person earns in a lifetime. All the same, there is a difference of scale between advertising and TV: a creative designer can take a year to make a thirty-second film whereas a TV producer can take thirty seconds conceiving a whole series.

And being a creative designer isn't an easy job. Its reputation has suffered because of its apparent simplicity. Everyone thinks they could do it. This morning's meeting should give you some idea of how difficult the job is, though. If we pursue our comparison between a copywriter and a freelancer on the *Guardian*, it would be like telling the journalist that his article would be rewritten by the assistant editor, then the editor, then the editorial director, then re-read and altered by every person mentioned in his text, then read in public to a representative sample of the newspaper's readership, before being modified again, and even then it would only have a 10 per cent chance of being published in the end. Do you know many journalists who'd agree to be treated like that? That's another reason we're so well paid.

All these ads that you see everywhere do actually have to be made up by someone somewhere along the line. The chairman of the agency and his commercial directors sell them to their advertising clients, they're talked about in the press, they're parodied on the box, they're dissected by media students, they increase the notoriety of the product and its sales figures in one go. But at some point, there's a young prick sitting on his chair who dreamed them up in his little head, and that young prick is worth a lot, I mean really a lot, because he's the Master of the Universe, as I've already explained. This young prick is at the very extremity of the productivist chain, where all industry leads, where the war of economics is at its most intense. The brands come up with products, millions of workers manufacture them in factories, they're distributed round countless shops. But all this fuss wouldn't mean a thing if the young prick on the chair didn't find a way of crushing the competition, winning the battle and convincing the buyers not to choose another brand. This war isn't just some gratuitous activity, and it's not a game for dilettantes. You don't do this sort of thing lightly or unadvisedly. There's almost a feeling of mysticism when I sit facing Charlie – another creative designer and my art director – and we feel, we know, that we've come up with yet another idea which will flog some useless product to every unfortunate housewife in the land. We suddenly look at each other with a conspiratorial gleam. The magic has been done: making people who haven't got the means want to buy something they didn't need ten minutes earlier. Every time is like the first. The idea always comes from nowhere. It's a miracle which bowls me over again and again; it brings tears to my eyes . . . God, I really do urgently need to be turfed out.

My exact title is 'advertising copywriter'; that's what we call public writers nowadays. I dream up thirty-second film scripts and slogans for posters. I say 'slogan' so that you know what I mean, but, let me tell you, the word 'slogan' is well past its sell-by date. We now say 'hook', and it sounds so much swankier. All the really snobby copywriters say 'hook', so I do it too. I go around saying I came up with this or that 'hook', because if you're a snob you're more likely to get a raise. I'm working on eight accounts: a French perfume, an outdated brand of clothing, an Italian pasta, an artificial sweetener, a mobile phone, a fat-free fromage frais, an instant coffee and a carbonated orange drink. My days are spent zapping between these eight different balls, keeping them all in the air. I'm a chameleon soaring through space as high as a kite (mixing metaphors goes with the territory).

I know you're not going to believe me when I tell you this, but I didn't choose the job just for the money. I like putting sentences together. No other job gives so much power to individual words. An advertising copywriter writes aphorisms for a living. However much I may hate what I've become you can't get away from the fact that there's no other job in which people can argue for three weeks about the use of one adverb. When Cioran wrote, 'I dream of a world where people would die for one comma', did he realize he was talking about our world, the copywriters' world?

Copywriters work in a team with an art director. They too have found a little phrase to set them apart: they call themselves 'ADs' (and all over the world they use this English-language abbreviation, even if it bears no relation to their own language). Right, I'm not going to go into every single little foible in advertising, that's not what we're here for. If that's what you're after just watch re-runs of 1970s comedy programmes like *Reginald Perrin*, the sort of stuff they put on on Sunday evenings. People used to laugh about advertising, but no one's laughing about it any more. It no longer seems like a cheerful adventure, it's a cold and invincible industry. Working in an ad agency has become about as exciting as being a chartered accountant.

Basically, the days when advertisers could pass themselves off as entertainers are over. Now they're seen as dangerous, calculating, implacable businessmen. The general public is beginning to cotton on and they go a long way to avoid our exposure: not looking at the screens, tearing up the prospectuses, steering clear of the bus stops and spraying graffiti over the hoardings. This reaction is called 'ad-phobia'. While no one was looking, all the different tentacles of advertising ended up running the whole show. Something that started as a joke now dominates our lives. It finances the television, dictates what's printed in the papers, governs sport (when everyone thought France beat Brazil in the World Cup, what really happened was that Adidas beat Nike), shapes society, influences sexuality and encourages inflation. You want some figures? The global investment in advertising in 1998 was £234 billion (that's a lot of money, whichever currency you put it in). I can assure you that, at that sort of price, everything is for sale – especially your soul.

8

I keep rubbing my gums; they itch like crazy. As I get older my lips are getting thinner and thinner. I'm up to four grams of cocaine a day. It starts as soon as I wake up. I have my first line before my early morning cup of coffee. It's a shame we have only two nostrils, otherwise I'd take a lot more of the stuff at a time. Coke is a 'stress-buster', according to Freud. It anaesthetizes problems.

Why do the Americans control the world? Because they control our means of communication. I came to this American agency because I knew Mark Browning worked here. The agency is called Rosserys & Crow but everyone calls it The Ross. I work for the British subsidiary of the first world-wide advertising company, founded in New York in 1947 by Ed Rossery and John Crow (they cumulated a gross margin of $5.2 billion in 1999). The offices must have been built in the early 1980s: that ocean-liner look was in at the time. There's a big central courtyard and yellow pipe-work pretty much all over the place. It's somewhere between a mini Pompidou Centre and Alcatraz, but it's actually in Soho, which doesn't have the kudos of Madison Avenue. The vast initials R & C dominate the entrance lobby, surrounded by rich – plastic – foliage. Men walk past briskly with files under their arms. Nubile girls talk into mobile phones. They all feel they have a mission: rekindling the image of a toilet paper, launching a new powdered soup, 'consolidating the optimized position achieved last year in the margarine sector', 'exploring new territories for salami' . . . I once came across a pregnant marketing executive crying in a corridor (marketing executives go and hide if they need to cry). I played the role of helpful passer-by: I offered her a glass of water, a tissue, a hand on her arse. Nothing doing: she forced a smile but I could tell that she was ashamed of having cracked up in front of someone.

'Last night I dreamed that my feet had a mind of their own, and they were walking me to The Ross. I tried to fight against them, but they were on auto-pilot . . . But I'm fine, really, it's nothing, it'll pass.'

She asked me not to mention it to her boss, reassured me that she felt absolutely fine, that it was nothing to do with her job but the pregnancy was making her feel tired, that was all. She put some more make-up on and scrammed as fast as she could. That was how I came to realize that I was a full-time salaried member of an inhuman sect which turned pregnant women into rusting robots.

Mark Browning has just slapped my hand in greeting.

'Hello, skiver! Still writing your book at the company's expense, trying to bring advertising to its knees?'

'What do you mean! You taught me everything I know!'

The sad thing is it's true. Browning is creative director at The Ross but he still manages to write books, appear on television, get divorced, write book reviews in a controversial weekly . . . He does a load of stuff and he encourages his employees to do as much, to give them an 'open mind' (that's the Browning version, but I know it's to stop them going out of their minds). Browning's pretty much finished in this profession, but in his time he was a real winner: Golden Lions in Cannes, on the cover of *Campaign*, first prize at the CD & AD Club . . . He devised quite a few catchy baselines: 'LOOK ME IN THE EYE, I SAID IN THE EYE' for Wonderbra, 'TIME FLIES WHEN YOU'RE ENJOYING YOURSELF' for Virgin Atlantic, 'PUT UP OR SHUT UP' for Multiyork sofabeds and, his most famous one, 'NESCAFÉ. THERE'S PROBABLY A BETTER COFFEE. SHAME IT DOESN'T EXIST'. Christ, it seems so simple but you have to find it. The more simple they are, the harder they are to flush out. Some of the best strap-lines are disarmingly obvious: 'IT'S GOOD TO TALK', 'BECAUSE I'M WORTH IT', 'NEVER KNOWINGLY UNDERSOLD', 'SIMPLY YEARS AHEAD', '100% OF THE WINNERS TRIED THEIR LUCK', 'BREAD'S BETTER WI' NOWT TAKEN OUT', 'IT DOES EXACTLY WHAT IT SAYS ON THE TIN', 'LIP REPAIR NOT LIP SERVICE', 'CHOCOLATES? MALTESERS!' and, of course, 'JUST DO IT', the best one in the history of the business. (Mind you, on reflection, my favourite is still 'HYUNDAI. PREPARE TO WANT ONE'. It's the most honest. When they used to torture prisoners, they would say, 'We have ways of making you talk'; now they say, 'We have ways of making you want.' The pain is worse because it goes on so much longer.)

Browning knows all the ins and outs of the profession.

He taught me the unwritten laws, the ones you'll never learn on any marketing course. I took the liberty of printing them out on to a sheet of A4, which I've pinned above my iMac.

THE COPYWRITER'S TEN COMMANDMENTS

1) A good copywriter never targets the consumer but the twenty people most likely to employ him (the creative directors of the twenty best advertising agencies). Consequently, winning prizes in Cannes or at the CD & AD Club is far more important than winning market share for a client.

2) The first idea is the best, but you should always insist that you need three weeks before you can do a presentation.

3) Advertising is the only job in which you're paid for doing things badly. When you present the client with a brilliant idea and they want to 'make a few alterations', think long and hard about your salary, then cobble together the crap they're dictating in thirty seconds flat and chuck a few palm trees in on the storyboard so that you can go and spend a week in Miami or Capetown for the filming.

4) Always arrive late for meetings. A copywriter who arrives on time loses all his credibility. When you come into the room (where everyone's been waiting for you for three-quarters of an hour) avoid apologizing at all costs and just say, 'Hello, everyone, I've only got a few minutes.' Or quote from Roland Barthes: 'It's not the dream that sells, it's the meaning.' (The other option, which isn't quite so chic, is to quote from Raymond Loewy: 'Ugly doesn't sell well.') The clients will think they're getting their money's

worth. Never forget that advertisers go to agencies because they don't have ideas of their own. They feel as if
they've failed and they resent us for having ideas for them.
That's why copywriters should feel nothing but contempt
for them: product managers are masochistic and jealous.
They pay us to humiliate them.

5) When you haven't prepared anything, always be the last
to speak and take the credit for what everyone else has
said. In any meeting it's always the last person to speak
who's right. Never lose sight of the fact that the purpose
of a meeting is to give everyone else a chance to make an
arse of themselves.

6) The difference between a senior and a junior is that the
senior is better paid and works less. The more you're
paid, the more people listen to you, and the less you
speak. In this line of business, the more important you
are, the more effort you should make to keep your mouth
shut – because the less you say, the more people respect
you. The corollary of that is: in order to sell an idea to the
creative director, a copywriter should *systematically* lead
the CD to believe that it was he who had the idea in the
first place. To achieve this he should start his presentations along these lines: 'I've thought a great deal about
what you told me yesterday . . .' or 'In response to your
idea the other day . . .' or even 'I've gone back to your
original line of thinking, and . . .' Of course, it goes without saying that the CD didn't say anything yesterday,
didn't have any ideas the other day, and didn't have any
specific line of thinking in the first place.

Another way of distinguishing between a junior and a

senior: the junior tells funny jokes which no one laughs at, while his boss makes pathetic gags that have everyone pissing themselves.

7) Cultivate absenteeism, come to work at noon, never answer when people say hello, take three hours for lunch, and make sure no one can get hold of you on your extension. If anyone has a go at you about this, say, 'Copywriters don't work to a timetable, just to a deadline.'

8) Never ask anyone their opinion on a campaign. If you ask anyone their opinion, there's always a *chance* that they'll give it. And once they've given it, it's *highly probable* that you'll have to act on it.

9) Everyone does the work of the person above them. The work-experience girl does the work of the copywriter, who does the work of the creative director, who does the work of the chairman. The more important you are, the less work you do (see the Sixth Commandment). One high-flyer, let's call him Travis Botty, lived for twenty years on the back of a campaign that was actually put together by another guy, Mick Wank for the sake of argument, and he got it from the work of two agency copywriters whose names have been completely forgotten. People are always taking credit for the work of their underlings. *Pass on* all your work to your work-experience boy: if it goes down well, take the credit; if it stinks, he'll get the elbow. They're our new slaves: they're not paid, they can be exploited mercilessly, fired from one day to the next, and used as coffee-making machines and walking photocopiers – they're as dispensable as a Bic razor.

10) When a copywriting colleague submits a good ad to you, whatever you do don't show that you like what they've come up with. You should tell them it's a load of crap, unsaleable, or that it's old hat: it's been done hundreds of times before or it's straight out of some foreign campaign. When they show you an ad that really is a load of crap, you should say, 'I love your idea', and pretend to be really envious.

Now that Browning is managing the agency's creative work, he's forgotten all his precepts. When someone shows him an idea for a campaign, he grumbles, 'No'-ba'' or 'No'-shaw'. 'No'-ba'' means that he likes it and that its creator will be promoted before the end of the year. 'No'-shaw' means the guy's got to find something else on pain of being given the elbow within a fortnight. In short, there's no great mystery to the job of art director: you just have to know how to mumble 'no'-ba'' and 'no'-shaw' properly. I sometimes wonder whether Mark doesn't pronounce his judgements on a whim, by tossing a coin in his head.

He contemplated me with something akin to indulgence before interrupting my reverie.

''pparently you really fucked up at Damione this morning.'

So I gave him this great tirade, rattling it out on my keyboard at the same time so that you could have the opportunity to read it.

'Listen, Mark, you should know, *all* copywriters end up going mad. The work's just too frustrating, you get everything chucked back in your face, it's getting worse and worse. This agency's biggest client is the bin! God, the work we do for the bin! Look at the resigned expression on the faces of the older people who work here, not a shred of hope left in their eyes. Once you've had a certain number of ideas turned down, you start to get the picture and even if you pretend not to mind, it gets to you. We're all failed artists, anyway, then we have to swallow our pride and fill our drawers with rejected dummies. You'll say: it's better than working in a factory. But at least there they know they're making something tangible, whereas anyone 'creative' has to assume some high-blown title, a ridiculous name which only gives him the authority to build castles in the air and to prostitute his talents. And anyway, everyone who works here is either alcoholic, depressive or on drugs. By the afternoon, they're stumbling about the place, yelling at each other, playing video games for hours, smoking joints . . . We all have our ways of dealing with it. I even saw someone a few minutes ago pretending to be a tight-rope walker on a beam fifteen metres up from the ground. In my case, I've got such a noseful that I can't stop grinding my teeth, my face is overrun with twitches and my cheeks are sweating. But, in the name of this pathetic cohort, I proclaim the following: my book will avenge every assassinated idea.'

Browning is listening to me compassionately, like a doctor preparing to tell his patient that the result of his HIV test is positive. When I've said my piece, he pauses before adding his.

'You'll just have to resign,' he says, walking out of my office.

Stuff it, I'm going to persevere, I'm not resigning. That would be like throwing in the towel before the end of a boxing match. I'd rather end up being knocked out and taken off on a stretcher. Anyway, he's lying. No one here would let me just slam the door on the place. If I left it would be like in *The Prisoner*, they'd never stop questioning me: 'Why did you leave?' I've always wondered why the people who ran the village kept asking Number 6 that question. Now I know. Because that really is the big question of the century, in a world terrorized by unemployment and totally geared to the cult of full-time work: 'WHY DID YOU LEAVE YOUR JOB?' I remember every time the credits rolled, I was impressed by Patrick McGoohan's sardonic smile as he shouted, 'I am not a number, I'm a free man!' We're all Number 6 now. We're all fighting to get permanent contracts. And if you do chuck in your work and head off to the salvation of a desert island with whores trashed on cocaine, that great white ball could come bobbing on to the beach at any moment to bring you back to the office: 'WHY DID YOU LEAVE?'

9

At the time we used to put gigantic photographs of products on walls, bus stops, houses, the ground, taxis, lorries, the scaffolding on buildings that were being restored, furniture, lifts, ticket machines, in every street and even in the country. Every aspect of life was invaded by bras, frozen foods, anti-dandruff shampoo and razors with three blades. The human eye had never been so solicited. It was estimated that in their first eighteen years, every person would be exposed to an average of 350,000 advertisements. Even on the edge of forests, in the middle of tiny villages, in the depths of isolated valleys and on top of the snow-capped mountains, on the cable cars themselves, you would have to confront logos from Marlboro, Microsoft, Badedas and Pretty Polly. Not a moment's rest for the retina of *Homo consumiens*.

Silence was also on its way out. You couldn't get away from the radios, the blaring televisions, the jangling commercials which even infiltrated private telephone conversations. That was a new tariff introduced by a telephone server desperate for market share: free calls in exchange for ten-second commercial breaks. Just imagine it: the telephone rings, a policeman tells you that your child has just died in a car crash, you dissolve into tears and the voice on the other end of the line says, 'Mouth ulther? Bonjela!' There was lift music everywhere, and not just in the lifts. Mobile phones trilled on the train, in restaurants, in churches, and even Benedictine monasteries found it difficult to resist the ambient cacophony. (I know: I checked.) According to the research cited above, the average Westerner was subject to 4,000 commercial messages a day.

Man had gone into Plato's cave. He was the Greek philosopher who envisaged men chained in a cave, watching the shadows of reality playing out on the walls of their dungeon. Plato's cave really did exist now: it was called television. On the screen of our cathode ray tube we could contemplate a Canada Dry reality: it was like reality, it was the same colour as reality, but it wasn't reality. The Greek *logos* had been replaced by logos projected on to the damp walls of our grotto.

It took us 2,000 years to end up like that.

and now a page of advertising script . . .

The scene is set in Jamaica.

Three rastas are lying under a coconut palm, their faces almost hidden by their dreadlocks. They've obviously smoked loads of ganja and are completely stoned.

A big black woman comes over and calls out, 'hey, boys, it's time to go to work!'

The three reggae men don't move a muscle. They're obviously too wrecked to lift so much as a little finger. They smile at her and shrug their shoulders, but the fat mama won't give up.

'Get up! That's enough! Get to work!'

Seeing that the three 'brothers' still aren't going to move, she brandishes a pot of Yoplite in desperation. When they see the creamy chocolate pudding, the three rastamen get to their feet instantly, singing Bob Marley's 'Get Up, Stand Up'. They dance around on the beach as they spoon the product into their mouths.

Packshot of Yoplite with the signature: 'Everyone gets up for a Yoplite'.

2 You

'The things you discover in Pascal's *Pensées* are no more precious than those you discover in a soap advertisement.'

Marcel Proust

10

Another sleepless night. Since Sophie left, you're always bored at the weekend. It was meant to be invigorating going solo, but you didn't know you'd be going so low. You gaze vacantly at *The Grind* on MTV. Thousands of girls in bikinis and skimpy T-shirts jigging on a huge open-air dance floor, probably on South Beach in Miami. Muscly black blokes corral them with their gleaming chocolate-bar abdomens. The programme has no concept beyond plastic beauty and techno sweat. Everyone has to be sixteen for ever. You have to be young, beautiful, sporty, tanned, smiling and in time to the music. Enjoy yourself, fine, but make sure you're disciplined and obedient in the glorious sunshine. Skin-tight clothes are compulsory. *The Grind* is another world, perfection on a beach, dance in all its purity. Just think about the word GRIND ([graìnd] *vb* 1. to reduce or be reduced to small particles by pounding or abrading). Their enforced fasting reminds you of Leni Riefenstahl's *Triumph of the Will* or Arno Breker's sculptures.

Every now and again in the background, an exhausted girl who doesn't realize that she's on camera starts yawning. Then the camera comes closer and as soon as she sees the lens she goes back to her prick-teasing antics, posing like a

porn actress and sucking her fingers with affected innocence. For a whole interminable hour you watch this
beach-side fascism while you sniff your coke. To stop your
nose bleeding, you take a long time crushing the powder on
the mirror with your ultra-platinum credit card. You turn
the crystals into icing sugar. The finer the powder, the less
it irritates the blood vessels. Your life is set along these
lines. Once you've inhaled them with your solid-gold
straw, you tip your head backwards so that your sinuses
don't get too involved in the procedure. As soon as you get
the taste of it in your throat, you drink a big vodka and
tonic to stop the endless sneezing. After hay fever, you
inaugurate a new illness: coke fever (necrosis of the nostrils,
runny nose, twitching jaw, corroded Visa card with a
whitened edge). That's how you spend the whole weekend
floating somewhere above yourself.

Drugs. You've watched as they gradually inveigled their
way into your life. At first you only heard people talking
about it.

'We had some charlie this weekend.'

Then some friends of friends passed some around.

'D'you want a line?'

Then your friends' friends became your dealers.

Next thing you know, one of them's died of an overdose
and the other one's landed in jail. At first you took it just
for fun, every now and again. Then to help you relax every
weekend. Then to help you keep your sense of humour
during the week. Then you forgot that it made you laugh,
and you settled for taking some every morning just to stay
normal. And it makes you want to crap when it's cut with

laxatives, and your nose itches like fury when it's cut with strychnine. You don't complain: if you weren't sniffing the marching powder, you'd have to go bungee-jumping in fluorescent-green jump-suits, or roller-blading in monstrous knee pads, or do karaoke in a Chinese restaurant, or get racist with the skinheads, or do exercises in the gym with all the mutton dressed as lamb, or the National Lottery on your own, or psychoanalysis with a couch, or poker with a bunch of liars, or surfing on the Internet, or sado-masochism, or a weight-loss diet, or closet whisky drinking, or gardening, or cross-country running, or urban stamp-collecting, or bourgeois Buddhism, or pocket multi-media, or group home-improvements, or anal orgies. Everyone needs some activity to 'de-stress' as they say, but you know it's not just a coincidence that the word sounds strangely like 'distress'. They're not waving, they're drowning.

Since you've been living on your own, you wank too much in front of the video. You've always got bits of tissue stuck to your fingers. And yet when you dumped Sophie you told her you preferred prostitutes.

'I'm faithful to you: you're the only person that I feel like cheating on.'

Hang on, how did it happen? Oh yes, you were having dinner with her in a restaurant, when she suddenly announced that she was pregnant and the baby was yours. This flashback is not a good memory. Suddenly you launched into a long, unstoppable monologue. You ranted at her, saying all the things men all over the world dream of saying to their pregnant girlfriends.

'I really want us to break up . . . I'm sorry . . . Please don't cry . . . There's only one thing I want and that's for us to go our separate ways . . . I'll die alone like a shit . . . Piss off, get out of my face, go and rebuild your life while you're still pretty . . . Don't come near me any more . . . I've tried, believe me, I've tried to hang on, but I won't make it . . . I'm suffocating, I can't cope with this any more, I don't know how to be happy . . . I just want to be on my own, no strings attached . . . I want to travel abroad as a single man . . . I couldn't possibly bring up a child, I *am* one myself . . . I am my own son . . . Every morning I give myself the gift of life . . . I didn't *have* a father, how do you expect me to *be* one? . . . I don't want your love . . . I . . .'

That seemed like a lot of sentences beginning with 'I'.

Sophie replied, 'You're . . . you're a monster.'

'If I'm a monster and you love me, that makes you about as intelligent as the bride of Frankenstein.'

Sophie scanned your face and then got up and walked out of your life without even drawing breath. And it's weird but, as she left in tears, you were well aware that you were the one who was actually running away. You breathed in and out again; you felt the relief of the 'easy option' that goes with every separation; you jotted on the paper table-cloth: 'Break-ups are love's Munichs' and 'What others call tenderness I call fear of splitting up' and also 'With women it's always the same. Either you don't give a damn about them or you're afraid of them.' If you do give a damn, then you must be terrified.

When a girl tells her man that she's pregnant, the

question that *immediately* comes to his mind isn't, 'Do I want this baby?' but 'Am I going to stay with this girl?'

At the end of the day, freedom is just a difficult period you have to get through. This evening you've decided to go back to Lola's Bar, your favourite brothel. These establishments are meant to be illegal in Britain, but there are at least five hundred in London alone. In this one, as soon as you go through the door, the girls are all over you. They have two points massively in their favour:

1) They're gorgeous.
2) They don't belong to you.

You order a bottle of bubbly, offer it to everyone and suddenly there they are stroking your hair, licking your neck, insinuating their fingernails under your shirt, skimming their hands over your swelling fly-zip and murmuring sweet obscenities in your ear:

'You're so cute, I really want to suck you. Oh, Sonia, look, isn't he gorgeous! I can't wait to see his face when he comes in my mouth. Put his hand in my panties so he can feel how wet I am. My clit's quivering. There, can you feel it throbbing against your finger?'

You take them at their word. You forget you're paying them. In your heart of hearts you're pretty sure that Joella's real name is Joanna, but until you've come you couldn't care less. You're like a horse in clover . . . and the girls can spread it on straight from the fridge. There you are in the basement of Lola's Bar, suckling on silicone breasts. They mother you. Long, languishing tongues lick across your face. You justify your actions out loud.

'When your car needs repairing, it's best to call on a mechanic. To build a house, the recommended course of action is to use a good architect. If you fall ill, you should consult a competent doctor. Why should physical love be the only domain in which we don't have recourse to specialists? We're all prostitutes. Ninety-five per cent of people would agree to sleep with someone if they were offered £1,000. Any girl would probably give you a blow-job for half that price. She'd pretend to be upset by the suggestion, she wouldn't boast about it to her friends, but I think for £500 you could do what you wanted with her. For less even. You can have whoever you want, it's just a question of price. Would you refuse to suck someone's dick for a million, two million, 100 million? Love's a hypocrite most of the time. Pretty girls fall in love (and they truly believe their love is totally sincere) with guys who just happen to be loaded and who are most likely to be in a position to offer them a life of luxury. Are you trying to tell me that's not prostitution? Of course it is.'

Joella and Sonia concur with your reasoning. They always agree with your brilliant theories. Birds of a feather flock together – you see, you too have sold your soul to major investors.

Incidentally, these girls are the only thing that manage to give you a hard-on even with your nose filled to the gunnels and a condom on your dick, when you're in such a state all you can do is announce, 'Look not unto the straw in thy neighbour's nose but rather unto the oak beam within thine own trousers.'

You like to think you're provocative and you've seen it

all before, but that's not you at all. You don't use prostitutes out of cynicism, indeed not; on the contrary, it's because you're afraid of love. They give you sex without emotion, pleasure without pain. 'Truth is a part of what is false,' wrote Guy Debord – after Hegel – and both of them were more intelligent than you are. That sentence describes hostess bars very well. With prostitutes everything that is false is part of the truth. You are yourself at last. When you're with a so-called 'normal' woman, you have to try so hard; show yourself off to good effect; improve yourself – lie, basically: that's how men prostitute themselves. Whereas in a brothel, men can just let themselves go, they don't have to make any effort to please anyone or to try to be better than they really are. It's the only false place where men can finally be true, weak, beautiful and vulnerable. Someone should write a novel called *Love Costs £300*.

The whores are a pretty expensive way of economizing. You're too soft to risk falling in love again, and all that it entails: galloping heart, high emotions, sudden disappointments, Wuthering Heights. Nothing seems more romantic to you than going to the brothel. Only truly sensitive creatures have to pay to avoid the risk of suffering.

Once they're past thirty everyone protects themselves. After a few heartbreaks, women flee any further danger, they go out with safe, reassuring, boring older men; men don't want to love anyone any more, they set themselves up with Lolitas or whores; everyone covers themselves with a tough shell; no one ever wants to feel stupid or unhappy again. You wish you could go back to the days when love didn't hurt. When you were sixteen you would go out with girls and dump them or they would walk out on you without any problem, in two minutes the whole thing was over. Why does everything become so much more important later? Logically it should be the other way round: dramas in adolescence, flippancy in your thirties. But that's not what it's like. The older you get the softer you get. You're too serious when you're thirty-three.

Afterwards, when you get home, you take a sleeping pill and you no longer ever dream. It's only then, my poor boy, that just for a few hours, you manage to forget Sophie.

11

On Monday morning you arrive at The Ross with a heavy heart. You can't help thinking about the merciless selection of the marketing king. Once upon a time there were sixty different varieties of apple: now there are only three left (Golden Delicious, those green ones and the red ones). Once upon a time it took chickens three months to reach maturity; now from the hatching of the egg to the vacuum-packed chicken in the hypermarket there are just forty-two days in appalling conditions (twenty-five of them per square metre, all fed on antibiotics and tranquillizers). Until the 1970s there were ten distinctly different varieties of Normandy Camembert; now there are three at the out-side (because of the homogenizing effects of heat-treating the different milks). This may not be your doing but it is your world. They no longer put cocaine in Coca-Cola (£1 billion spent on advertising in 1997), but why won't they tell you what *is* in it? You can be sure there's a good reason. (I know, but my publisher won't let me tell you.) Dairy cattle are fed on fermenting silage which gives them cirrhosis of the liver; cattle are also dosed with antibiotics which create strains of resistant bacteria, and these end up on the meat counter (and that's without going into the animal-based feeds which provoke bovine spongiform encephalitis, but we won't rake up that again). The milk from these same cows contains more and more dioxins because the grass on which they graze is contaminated. The stringent restrictions the supermarkets impose on abattoirs mean that animals are trundled up and down the country to be slaughtered (and look what fun foot and mouth had with that!). Farmed fish are fed on fish meal (as noxious to them as the animal-based feeds are for cows) and antibiotics. In winter there's no danger that the transgenic strawberries will freeze thanks to a gene borrowed from a fish which thrives in sub-zero temperatures. Genetic manipulations mean that chicken characteristics are being introduced into potatoes, scorpion characteristics into cotton, hamster into tobacco, tobacco into lettuce and human into tomatoes.

At the same time, more and more people in their thirties suffer from cancer of the kidney, the uterus, the breast, the anus, the thyroid, the intestine and the testicles, and doctors don't understand why. Even children are affected: increased incidence of leukaemia, a new upsurge in brain tumours, repeated epidemics of bronchitis in cities . . . According to Professor Montagnier (who discovered the HIV virus), the advent of AIDS is explained not only by the transmission of the virus but also by other 'lifestyle-related' factors, such as pollution and diet, which break down our immune system. The quality of sperm is degenerating every year; human fertility is under threat.

This whole civilization rests on the false longings that you dream up. It's going to die. Our way of life is a big suicide.

In your place of work there's a lot of information available to you. You learn, quite incidentally, that there are such things as unbreakable washing machines which no manufacturer wants to launch on the market; that some bloke has invented tights that don't ladder but one of the big hosiery brands has bought his patent in order to destroy it; that a puncture-proof tyre is also tucked in a drawer somewhere (and this is at the cost of thousands of fatal accidents a year); that the oil-producing countries are lobbying frantically to delay the widespread introduction of electric cars (and the cost here is the continued increase in carbon dioxide gases in the atmosphere, causing global warming, or the 'greenhouse effect', which will probably be responsible for a whole series of natural disasters in the next fifty years: hurricanes, melting of the icecaps, raising of the sea level, skin cancers, and that's before you even consider the oil slicks); that even toothpaste is a superfluous product because dental health relies entirely on the brushing, the paste serves only to freshen the breath; that all washing powders, liquids and dinky little tablets are interchangeable, and besides, it's actually the machine which does the washing; that CDs get scratched just as easily as vinyl; that tin foil is more contaminated than asbestos; that the formula for sun creams has remained unchanged since the war, despite the increase in malignant melanomas (sun creams protect only against UVB rays but not harmful UVA rays); that Nestlé's advertising campaign encouraging Third World mothers to fill their babies with powdered milk caused millions of infant deaths (the parents were mixing the powder with undrinkable water).

The glorious reign of merchandise is dependent on sales. Your job is to convince consumers to choose the product that will be used up the fastest. Manufacturers call this 'programming obsolescence'. You will be asked to turn a blind eye and to keep your opinions to yourself. Yes, you could do a Neville Chamberlain, you could always claim that you didn't know, or that you didn't have any choice, or that you tried to slow down the process, or that no one could force you to be a hero . . . There's no getting away from the fact that every day for ten years you didn't do a thing. If it weren't for you things could have happened differently. We might even have been able to imagine a world without the ever-present posters, villages without ugly-as-sin signs, street corners without fast-food outlets, and some actual people in those streets. People who talk to each other. Life didn't have to work out like this. You didn't want all this manufactured unhappiness. You didn't actually build all these cars (there are so many of them now – an estimated 2.5 billion by the year 2050 – that the 'mobile' bit of automobile no longer really applies, the motorways are giant car parks). But you did nothing to try to redecorate the world. One of the Ten Commandments in the Bible says: 'Thou shalt not make unto thee any graven image, or any likeness . . . thou shalt not bow down thyself to them.' Just like the whole of the rest of the world, you've been caught red-handed committing a mortal sin. And we all know the divine punishment: the Hell in which you live.

'Have you got a window so that I can debrief you or are you overbooked?'

Jeffrey, the commercial director on the Damione account, has just popped his head round your door.

'Charlie's buying artwork, it would be better early afternoon.'

'OK,' he says. 'I'm sure you will have guessed that you've got to fill out that Yoplite campaign. Going to have to calm things down a bit there.'

'Seduction, seduction, that's what we're after. It's the only thing that matters. It's what drives everything people do.'

He looks at you oddly.

'Tell me, are you sure you got enough rest this weekend?'

'I'm ready to get my teeth into a new week in my role as henchman to this spectacular society. Long live the Fourth Reich!'

Jeff comes over towards you and stares at the end of your nose.

'You've got something white there.'

(What you need is something that 'works fast and leaves no powdery residue'.)

He dusts your frosted nostrils with the back of his sleeve, then goes on, 'I might be in another meeting later, but you can always get hold of me on my mobile.'

'Oooh, Jeff, I love getting hold of you on your mobile.'

Later on Charlie returns and sits down opposite you. Charlie is like a rampart: he's as stocky as you are slight. Charlie is a happy man, so he's good at mimicking happiness. He has a wife and two children; he sees life in a constructive light – to each his own way of dealing with this universal absurdity. Charlie forgives you your excesses. You like Charlie because he compensates for you. He smokes joints while you're busy wiping out your nerve endings. He spends his days tracking down the most obscene pornographic images on the Internet: a woman sucking off a horse, for example; a man nailing his balls to a plank of wood; a great fat woman fisted by a plastic arm – he finds them 'entertaining'.

'Do you know *The Grind* on MTV? I think we could really do something with that cattle-market. So many people, so little emotion, all that superficial beauty.'

Charlie nods at you approvingly as he rolls his joint.

'Yeah, it's pretty different. We could suggest that Yoplite sponsor it. And for the ad we could choose twenty-second clips and just add their logo top right, instead of MTV . . .'

'Now that would be a coup! Watching all those young guns jigging about on the "Yoplite TV" channel! You could even get some of it on to CNN! And it could be relayed to an even wider market through a series of events and receptions under the joint brand "Grind-Yoplite"!'

'Yup, and, given that there are hours and hours of the stuff, we could broadcast a different sequence every day. It would be the first commercial that never repeated itself!'

'That would be great for the spin-offs in the press. Make a note of what you just said so that we can put it in the press release for the launch.'

'Fine, but how are we going to introduce the idea that "Yoplite makes you beautiful and intelligent"?'

'I've thought about that. So listen to this. You see thousands of kids dancing to house music, by a huge pool, under the electric blue sky. And suddenly, after twenty seconds, a sentence appears: "YOPLITE. AND YOU HAVEN'T HEARD THEM TALK YET".'

'Octave, you're a genius!'

'No, Charlie, you're the greatest!'

'I know.'

'So do I.'

'I could kiss you.'

'I love you for what you do.'

'Well, I love you for being *you*.'

You set to work on the new script while Charlie unearths a new video on the web: a man who's put a dildo on the end of a drill so that he can bore it into a pubescent girl while she sucks on her used tampon. Now that *is* entertainment.

The next day you take the new script up to Browning, who approves with a nod of his head (hardly surprising, he *is* the head).

'Just as unsaleable, but if it would amuse you to give it a whirl, go right ahead. All I ask, Octave, is that you don't do any more of your Charlie Manson-style graffiti on the premises of our valued client.'

Later, you contact the commercial director on his mo-vile phone.

'Jeffrey, we've got something.'

'Yippeka!'

(That's a contraction of 'Yippee.' and 'Eureka.' Good isn't it?)

'But we're going to need three weeks to work on it.'

Silence at the other end of the line.

'Are you guys crazy? I've got to show them something at the end of next week!'

'A fortnight.'

'Ten days.'

'Twelve.'

'Eleven.'

'Let's send him a VHS of the programme this afternoon,' Charlie says decisively. 'At Damione they're going to be so pleased that we've responded so quickly that they'll buy the idea without thinking.'

Jeff adds that 'it's a very product-oriented campaign based on a very brand-unifying idea' (end of quotation). You can't help clapping. Everyone says that the creative team feel only contempt for the commercial lot and that the feeling's mutual, but it's not true. They need each other, and in business you love the people you need; you only ever meet other people at their leaving dos. Charlie's well in control. And anyway, when Charlie's in a decisive mood, no one argues.

12

Sophie said goodbye to you as if she'd been saying hello.

You have lunch alone.

You used to have too many friends, now you don't have any.

Which means you never really had any.

You drink, your clothes stink of Thai curry.

How cool is that?

'Let me leave you, let me go, let me go back to being a young prat,' you said to her.

You go out without your glasses on so that you can only see a metre in front of you.

Your short-sightedness is your last luxury. Everything is wonderfully hazy, like in a pop video.

Everything is superficial.

Behave yourself.

You are at the pinnacle of consumer society and at the peak of communications society.

You order a sushi of pan-fried foie gras with Sechuan pepper and pear chutney in a veal-stock gravy with soya and balsamic vinegar.

There's a girl smiling at you.

You love her. She'll never know it.

Damn.

It was nice while it lasted.

You lean against the bar and dream about new women. You took your time working out what you wanted in life: solitude, silence, drinking, reading, taking drugs, writing and, every now and then, making love with a very pretty girl you'll never see again.

It was that time of day when creative directors go off for a blow-job. On the way back to the office you stop to buy yourself a bit of condom-free fellatio. Twenty minutes later you're back at the agency.

'Fire me!' you yell in the lobby at The Ross, but no one's listening. 'Fire me!'

A few trainees point at you and burst out laughing. They think you're joking and they take this opportunity to suck up to you (you've already established that it's that time of day) by guffawing loudly at your pathetic prank.

'Fire me!'

But in the impressive, airy, leafy open space of that lobby, there's no one to hear your cry. And you eventually realize why they're all giggling: there are traces of lipstick on the flies of your white jeans.

Your catch-phrases are trotted out on television all day long: 'IMITATE, DON'T INNOVATE', 'KENZO JUNGLE. JUST TRY TO TAME IT', 'VIAGRA. GIVE UP THE BRIDGE', 'EUROSTAR. ·WHY GO FROM HEATHROW TO ROISSY WHEN YOU CAN GO FROM LONDON TO PARIS?', 'BT. YOU ASKED FOR THE FUTURE? HOLD THE LINE', 'YSATIS DE GIVENCHY. LITTLE BLACK DRESS IN A

BOTTLE', 'MATES CONDOMS. IF YOU'RE UP FOR IT, WE'RE ON FOR IT', 'TOP SHOP. SO YOU, SO WHERE IT'S AT, SO WEAR IT!', 'ONE 2 ONE. MOUTH TO MOUTH RESUSCITATION', 'LOW-FAT EDAM. ALL THE FLAVOUR, HALF THE FAT – CLEVER CLOGS!'

'Fire me!'

You feel like lying down on a soft green lawn and crying up at the sky. It was advertising that got Hitler elected. Advertising is responsible for making people believe that their situation is normal when it isn't. Like medieval nightwatchmen, they seem to keep crying: 'Sleep, good people, it's midnight and all is well, the future's bright, the future's orange, stay special with Special K, Nivea – the feel good factor, Asda – permanently low prices for ever'. Sleep, good people. 'Everyone is unhappy in the modern world,' someone once said. Too right: the unemployed are unhappy because they don't have work, the employed are unhappy because they do. Sleep easy, take your Prozac. And whatever happens, don't ask any questions. *Hier ist kein warum.*

It has to be said that what goes on on the surface of this little planet is not very important on a galactic scale. The writings of an earthling will be read only by other earthlings. The other galaxies probably couldn't care less that Microsoft's annual turnover is equivalent to the GNP of Belgium, and that Bill Gates's personal fortune is estimated at $100 billion. You work, you become attached to other beings, you come to love a few places, but all you're doing is jumping up and down on a little pebble spinning in the dark. You can pack your pretensions away. Have you ever confronted the fact that you're about as important as a microbe? Haven't Glaxo-SmithKlein come up with a spray against pests like you?

You only listen to music by people who've committed suicide: Nirvana, INXS, Joy Division, Mike Brant. You feel old because you love listening to twelve-inch vinyl. In Britain there are nearly 12,000 suicides a year, that's more than one suicide every hour throughout the year. If you've been reading this book for an hour, *bang*, one person's died. Two hours if you read slowly? *Bang, Bang.* And so on. Over twenty-four voluntary corpses a day and 230 intentional interruptions of life a week. A thousand chosen deaths a month. Wholesale slaughter but no one talks about it. Britain is a sect of the huge Solar Temple. According to one survey, 13 per cent of British adults have 'seriously contemplated' killing themselves.

Every morning you consult four message services: your ansaphone at home, the one at work, your voice-mail box on your mobile and the e-mails on your iMac. Only your letter box stays soul-destroyingly empty. You don't get love letters any more. Never again will you get those sheets of paper covered in timid writing and impregnated with tears and perfumed with love and folded with such emotion and with the address written so carefully on the envelope and with a plea to the postman: 'Don't get lost on the way. Oh, my postman, take this important missive to its beloved recipient . . .' People are killing themselves because they don't get anything but advertisements through the post.

You give in to the temptations of UV. As soon as you feel depressed (the whole time, that is) you treat yourself to a session of ultraviolet. Which means the more blue you feel, the more bronzed you look. Sadness does your appearance no end of good. Despair is like sunshine for you. How can you hide the fact that you're miserable? You look fantastic. You think that being tanned means you can stay young when it's quite the reverse: the old and the has-beens are immediately recognizable by their permanent tans. Nowadays only the old have the time to go for gold. The young look pale and anxious but the old look tanned and happy (their retirement being paid for as it is by the former). Do you really want to look like that tragic case off *Dynasty*? You'll end up frazzling yourself with UV rays.

It was the best of lines, it was the worst of lines, it was the age of crystalline wisdom, it was the age of powdery foolishness . . . You had cocaine as an excuse. There are lots of things that you would never have dared do without it, like dumping Sophie or crucifying Dickens like that. Coke has broad shoulders. As you type this book out on your computer, you think of yourself as a secret agent who's infiltrated right into the heart of the system, a mole sent to spy on the mechanics of opinion-distortion. (After all, the CIA's an agency too, isn't it?) You're both a mercenary and a spy, amassing top-secret information on your hard drive. If you ever get caught, they'll torture you until you hand back the microfilms. You won't talk, you'll blame it on the drugs. When they hook you up to the lie-detector, you will swear to high heaven (high? – absolutely out of its tree) that your only part in this whole misadventure was as . . . a sentry.

Every day when you step out on to the street you see a

homeless man who looks just like you. The spitting image: tall, thin, pale with hollow cheeks. It's you with a beard, you dirty, you badly dressed, you smelling awful, you with your nose pierced, you without money, you with dog's breath, you very soon, you when the wheels have turned, you lying in the street above a hot-air outlet from the underground, your feet bare and bleeding. You don't buy the *Big Issue* from him. Sometimes he wakes and bellows at the top of his lungs, 'HE WHO SOWS THE WIND SHALL REAP THE WHIRLWIND!' then he goes back to sleep.

You spend entire nights in front of your PlayStation 2. For just £19.99 (all inclusive) you've joined the PlayStation club. Seven times a year you're sent 'demo CDs with purchase incentives and a questionnaire to help us at Sony gauge how many you already own, how many you would consider buying, how satisfied you are with the product, and any other comments you wish to make'.

You hang around at the supermarket for hours, smiling at the surveillance cameras. Another thing you've learned from your job: soon these cameras won't only be used for picking up shoplifters. Infra-red web-cams will be hidden in false ceilings and connected up to a central computer, so that the suppliers can keep track of your purchasing patterns by identifying the bar-codes of the items you select and by offering you promotions, by inviting you to try new products, and by making announcements over the PA system addressed specifically to you to send you to the departments you're most likely to need. Soon you won't even have to leave the house. The manufacturers will know your tastes because your fridge will be linked up to the

Net, and they'll come straight to your home to drop off the provisions you need, and your whole life will be indexed, recorded and industrialized. Wonderful, isn't it? Say hello to the camera. It's your only friend.

You've just received a brown A4 envelope. There, no need to despair: someone's written to you after all. You open it to find a strange black-and-white laser photocopy. A rudimentary sequence of letters is printed on it in a stark typeface, '43.5 0 bg4 fr15 pse12 rj33 gm f 2, alr l i/l ml dr55', with the time and date in the top left-hand corner. You're perplexed. By really studying the white blotches on the grey background you eventually make out a sort of extra terrestrial eye staring at you, two arms, the beginnings of a nose, something here that could be an ear ... You recognize it as an ultrasound scan. This work of abstract art is accompanied by a little hand-written note. 'This is the first and last time you will see your daughter. Sophie.'

73

13

A few days have gone by without you even noticing. Jeffrey imports his depression into your office.

'I've had some bad feedback from the advertiser. Alfred Dewler called after seeing the "Grind" tape to say that there were too many coloured people in it. He said, and I quote, "I'm not racist but the blacks make it too specific to one market, whereas we should be putting the emphasis on the Europeanness of the product. It's not my fault if the product is white and that, in order to sell it, we need to show white people. It's not racist to say that, for Christ's sake, we don't make black yoghurt! We'll use blacks when we bring out chocolate-flavoured Yoplite!"'

Apparently everyone burst out laughing when he said that. But he threatened to open the campaign up to tender again, which shut them up pretty quickly.

'Look, let's forget it,' you spit out. 'That fascist is the living incarnation of mediocrity. You should have reminded him that he's already producing a dioxin-flavoured Yoplite . . . He should use irradiated, disfigured, deformed, suppurating models.'

You're secretly delighted. Losing one of the agency's biggest budgets constitutes the fast-stream route for what you long for most, remunerated freedom, indefinite leisure time paid for by the company – paradise. But Jeffrey is already imagining himself on the streets. The situation is not the same for him as it is for you. He's been programmed for an existence without streets. He went to some daddy's-boy private business school, married a proper little bitch, agreed to be insulted and humiliated by his employers and his clients for fifteen years so that he could borrow money from the bank to buy a two-bedroom semi in the wrong end of Balham. His only form of relaxation? Listening to the soundtrack of *Titanic*. He can't imagine any other way of life. He's never left anything to chance. His life can't go down a different track. He would never recover if Damione stopped using the agency. He's almost in tears; this didn't feature in his career plan. For the first time in his life he doesn't know what to do. You never know, it might almost make him human.

'I know he's a fascist shit,' he mumbles, 'but he's worth a fortune . . .'

You start liking him. After all, he did dust your nose the other day.

'Don't worry,' you hear yourself telling him. 'We'll get them back for you, won't we, Charlie?'

'Yup. I think the time has come for us to go into DefCon Three alert.'

Mark Browning pops his head round the half-open door.

'Well, if you could see your faces! Anyone would think you worked for Rosserys & Crow . . . Ooops!'

He smacks his forehead with the palm of his hand.

'Oh, what a gaff! You do!'

'Stop mucking about, Mark,' says Jeff mournfully. 'We're in the shit right up to our necks on Yoplite.'

'Oh . . . they come on heavy, the guys who make the "lite" yoghurts . . .'

Browning shoots you a look of withering condescension (withering, that's him all over, but condescension? Condensation, more like, the wanker's full of hot air).

'Octave, Charlie,' he says, 'don't you think it's time to go into National Emergency mode?'

'They're already on DefCon Three!' exclaims Jeff. 'But, um . . . what exactly does this DefCon Three entail?'

That's when Charlie gives his solemn signal. He raises his eyes and his arms to the heavens, inhales deeply, exhales loudly – a sign that he's preparing either to speak or to kill some cute furry animal. After a long silence, he looks at Browning one last time.

'Boss? Do we have the green light?'

The boss nods his head before leaving the office, which is then bathed in a moment of almost Zen-like calm and serenity.

Charlie turns towards me slowly and utters the password: 'The Last-minute Cowpat.'

'All set.'

And before Jeff's very eyes, in one minute flat, you and Charlie concoct the commercial that all advertisers dream of: something sweet, gentle, inoffensive and deceitful aimed at a wide audience of mooing sheep (because, thanks to various genetic manipulations, it is now possible to make sheep moo).

You read the Cowpat out loud.

'A gorgeous woman (not too old, not too young), with *white skin*, mid-brown hair (not blonde, not dark), is sitting on the terrace of a lovely country house decorated *à la House Beautiful* (warm and welcoming but not garishly trendy) in a rocking chair (neither too expensive nor too old). She looks at the camera and says in a smooth but credible voice: **"Am I beautiful? People say so. But I don't even think about it. I'm just me."** Calmly (not sensuously or with too much sophistication) she picks up a pot of Yoplite and carefully begins opening it (not too quickly or too slowly), before tasting a spoonful (not a skimpy one but not a great big one). She closes her eyes with pleasure as she tastes the product (minimum two seconds). Then she goes on with her script, looking the viewer directly in the eye: **"My secret is. . . . Yoplite. A delicious fromage frais that's 100 per cent fat-free. With calcium, vitamins and protein. When you want to feel good in your head and your body, there's nothing better."** She gets up elegantly (but not too elegantly) and concludes with a conspiratorial smile (but not too conspiratorial): **"That's my secret. But it isn't a secret now, because I've told you. Ha ha."** She laughs mischievously (but not too mischievously). Then there's the packshot of the product (minimum five seconds) with this baseline: "YOPLITE. KEEPS YOU IN SHAPE, MIND AND BODY".'

Jeffrey went from devastated to euphoric in a split second: the man could get into the 'manic-depressive mime' department at RADA. He kisses our hands, our feet, our mouths.

'You've saved my life, my friends!'

'Now, now, no familiarities please,' grumbles Charlie, who's peering at the film on his computer screen: a man being sodomized by an eel.

As for you, you suddenly realize your mistake.

'Shit, now I'll never get the boot. With an ad like that, Philip'll be off my back for at least ten years. We're going to fuck Damione over again!'

But Charlie has the last word.

'You might say that you're fucking them over, but in your heart of hearts you know bloody well it's the other way round.'

And Jeffrey trots off merrily with his crappy script under his arm. This scene took place towards the beginning of the third century after the birth of Christ. (Now there was a hell of a copywriter, the author of many one-liners that are still famous to this day: 'LOVE ONE ANOTHER', 'TAKE, EAT, THIS IS MY BODY', 'FORGIVE THEM, THEY KNOW NOT WHAT THEY DO', 'THE FIRST SHALL BE LAST', 'IN THE BEGINNING WAS THE WORD' – oh, no, that was his father's).

14

Good cocaine costs £50 a gram. It's deliberately expensive, so that only rich people can feel good, while the poor go on destroying their livers with own-brand whisky.

You ring Tamara, your favourite call girl. Her answerphone greets you smoothly: 'If you want to ask me out for a drink, press 1. If you want to ask me out to dinner, press 2. And if you want to marry me, please hang up.' You leave your direct line at the agency, saying, 'Ring me back. I need your help to lighten up, urgently. Your shoulders are as smooth as boiled eggs and I want to dip my Marmite soldier in to you. Octave.' She has that sort of face . . . you just can't take your eyes off it.

Riddle: What has golden skin, a Mexican body and Eurasian eyes? Answer: A half-caste called Tamara. She's coming round to your place tonight. You've asked her to wear Obsession, Sophie's perfume.

She has a husky voice, slender fingers, mixed blood. A woman's body is made up of numerous elements that are not without charm: tanned tendons linking the ankles to the calves, painted toenails, a selection of dimples (corners of the mouth and top of the buttocks), teeth so white they contrast pleasingly with the dark red lips, various arches (bottom of the feet, small of the back), a variety of reds (cheeks, knees, heels, nipples), but the inside of the arm always stays as white as snow and as tender as the feelings it provokes.

Yes, it was a time when even tenderness was for sale.

Tamara is the whore that you don't fuck. Her miniskirt has the words 'LICK ME TILL I SCREAM' written across it, but you settle for licking her ear (she hates that). For £300, she'll sleep at your place. Before you used to listen to music together: Massive Attack, Daft Punk, Air. You're prepared to pay dearly just for that moment when your mouths are drawn together as if you loved each other. You don't want to sleep with her, just to run your hands over her, to feel her extraterrestrial attraction. Lovers are people who love each other. You refuse to put a condom inside Tamara. That's why you don't make love to her. At first, she couldn't understand this customer who seemed happy just rolling his tongue around hers. Then she learned to like it, the teeth nibbling her mouth, the nervy taste of saliva flavoured with vodka, and now she's the one who thrusts her tongue into your soft mouth, kissing you deeply, an oral penetration in which your tongue becomes your prick, licking her cheeks, her neck, her eyes, the taste, the sighs, the breathing, the titillated desire. Stop. You stop to smile at her from just one centimetre away. You know how to wait, to savour, to slow down and start again. It has to be said: a kiss is sometimes more wonderful than a fuck.

'I love your hair.'

'It's a wig.'

'I love your blue eyes.'

'They're lenses.'

'I love your breasts.'

'It's a Wonderbra.'

'I love your legs.'

'Ah! A compliment at last.'

Tamara bursts out laughing.

'You do make me laugh.'

'Does that mean you're happy?'

'At this precise moment? Yes.'

'At this precise moment, I know very well that you're faking it.'

'First of all, just because I'm not doing it for free doesn't mean I'm faking it. There's no connection. Secondly, yes, I am pretty happy – I'm making ten grand a month in cash.'

'Does money make you happy, then?'

'Not at all, but I'm putting a whole load aside to buy a house and bring up my baby.'

'What a shame. It would have been so nice to have made you unhappy.'

'I'm never unhappy when I make people pay.'

'It's the other way round for me. I pay you so as not to be unhappy.'

'Come on, kiss me. I'll give you ten per cent off this evening.'

She takes off her top. She has a fine gold chain round her waist and a rose tattooed above her right breast.

'Is that a real tattoo or a transfer?'

'A real one. You can suck it, it won't come off.'

Several magnetic encounters later, you film Tamara on your digital video camera and you interview her.

'Tell me, Tamara, do you really want to be an actress or was that a joke?'

'It's my dream, to do that sort of work as well as . . . this sort.'

'But why aren't you a model?'

'But I am, in the daytime. Like lots of the girls at Lola's Bar. I'm constantly going to castings. It's just there are so many girls and so little work that you have to find some way to make ends meet at the end of the month . . .'

'No, I was just asking because . . . Well, listen, here it is. I'd like to put you up for the next Yoplite ad.'

'OK, this evening I'll swallow your spunk for free.'

'No, no, come on. Don't you see? I'm the new Robin Hood.'

'What d'you mean?'

'It's so simple. I take from the rich to give to the girls.'

Yes, some evenings, you blew £300 just to kiss her in the rain and it was worth it. By Christ, it was worth it.

15

Ten days later it's the PPM at the agency, the Pre-production Meeting. The ultimate in meeting fever. You can't hear so much as a fly buzzing around the room. Hardly surprising – the flies probably know they'd be violently sodomized. Alfred Dewler's arrived with his three musketeers from Damione, there are two commercial directors from The Ross, the in-house TV producer, two creative designers (Charlie and myself), the film director we've booked for the job who's called Enrique Innizass, along with his producer, his depressive designer, his German set decorator and a cost controller with a face-lift. Charlie had a bet with me: the first one to use the expressions 'stress-inducing' and 'playing down' wins lunch at the Ivy.

'The modifications from our meeting of the 12th,' began the TV producer, 'have been integrated. We're waiting to do more castings but Enrique is OK with the agency's recommendations. So we'll go right ahead and show you the tape.'

But, as always happens in this sort of meeting, the video isn't working and no one knows how to use it. A technician has to be called, because the fourteen people in the room, representing a combined annual salary of over two million euros, are incapable of switching on a machine that a blind-folded six-year-old could operate with his left hand. While they wait for the arrival of the saviour (who will know how to press the 'play' button), the director reads aloud his objectives.

'The gerrel must-e not be too-e preetty, she must-e be fresh-looking, a yong adoolt.'

Enrique Innizass started out as a fashion photographer with *Glamour* before becoming the star director of man-nered advertising films bathed in an orange glow. He cultivates his Venezuelan accent because this exotic touch is the main reason for his success (there are about 500 out-of-work directors who film in exactly the same way as he does – i.e. in soft focus, using a profusion of filters and set to a trip-hop soundtrack – but they're not working because they're not called Enrique Innizass).

'I-a personally would-e be in favour of-e giving the brand-e name in-a the very first-e shot. Esta muy muy importante. But-e, we must-e steel leave ourselves-e room to be-a cree-ative, I sink.'

He was chosen because Jonathan Glazer wasn't free, and Tony Kaye wouldn't do it. Everyone follows their photo-copy of his notes with their fingers like nursery-school children. Suddenly a man in blue overalls comes in without knocking, sighs and switches on the video.

'Thank you, Jojo,' says Jeff, 'What would we be without you?'

'Useless twats,' mutters Jojo as he leaves the room.

Jeff forces a laugh.

'Ha, ha, ha! Good old Jojo. Right, so now we can watch the casting recommendation.'

So the fourteen useless twats watch the beautiful Tamara, naked to the waist except for her Wonderbra, looking into the camera as she bites her lips and says, 'It's my dream, to do that sort of work as well as . . . this sort. I'm constantly going to castings. Just there are so many girls and so little work . . . '

Cut.

You speak out quickly to say that this was an unofficial casting tape, an exceptional model whom you'd managed to film by chance, and that a call-back would be arranged the very next day to get the girl to read the exact script.

Alfred Dewler asks whether she could be touched up in post-production to lighten her skin colour.

'Of course, no problem. She'll be perfectly RWB!' (Red, white and blue).

His advertising director, a great fat slob in a Zara suit, opens his mouth for the only time in the whole meeting to utter these words: 'What we've got to do is arouse people's desires.'

Impressive, all these people who never get a fuck but who nevertheless work all day long to inflame the desires of millions of consumers.

The TV producer jots in her notebook: 'OK Tamara on condition of a call-back, and talk about using paintbox to lighten skin.'

Alfred Dewler speaks up again.

'I want to make it clear that we're delighted to be work-ing with Enrique, who's made a fantastic demo tape, and more particularly because we know that he is always extremely professional in his visual approach to advertising.'

(Simultaneous translation: 'We've chosen an easygoing director who won't change a thing in the script we've bought.')

'And Enrique, I appreciate what you're saying about the brand name. We all of us know that this isn't a poetry society. It's crucial that we identify the Damione logo properly in the very first shot of the ad.'

'Si, si. I-e thought-e I would-a do a very bright-e, glowing pack-e shot.'

'Quite,' agreed Jeff. ' The whole thing should have a sunny but clean feel to it.'

Then the designer chips in.

'We decided that it would be good if it wasn't too gloomy clothes-wise.'

She brandishes some brightly coloured T-shirts.

'We could find some reds, you know, flashy things like that.'

'Yes,' said one of the product managers, to justify his presence at the PPM (and, by extension, in the bosom of the Damione organization), 'of course, but we need mid-season styling so that we can use the film year-round.'

'In reference to what we said in our meeting of the 12th,' added the cost controller, who inspected all finished work carried out for Damione in order to criticize it and lower the fees (except her own), 'it needs to have a more impish, mischievous feel to it.'

'Obviously,' agreed Jeff, 'we made that clear on the 12th.'

They all look as if they're cracking under the pressure. The stylist has gone as red as her T-shirts.

'I brought this shirt along too . . .'

Everyone criticizes the shirt, until they realize the *client is wearing one* exactly like it.

'Listen,' says Charlie, 'we've got a basic contract but we can still allow ourselves a bit of spontaneity when we're filming, can't we?'

Everyone turns to look at Alfred-Dewler-is-a-prick.

'I must point out that Damione signs for a particular sequence and if we don't get that after the film's been edited, we throw it out. We have a contract. I think I've made myself clear on that point.'

'Of course,' quaked Jeff, 'the agency is doing everything it can to bring you back what we've shown you.'

And the conversation goes on like that for hours. Night falls. And you make notes on everything, scrupulously, like a clerk of the court – the scribe of our contemporary disaster. Because this meeting is more than a 'detail' in the history of the Third World War.

'Add the word "greedily" on the objectives for the filming. That's essential.'

'Do we really need thirty seconds? Couldn't we tell the story in twenty seconds if we made each shot shorter?'

'OK, we'll time the shots, but it could end up looking rushed.'

'It'll be hyper-cut.'

'So long as it doesn't affect the Ipsos allocation, I think we could do it as a twenty-second slot.'

'Put "irresistibly" instead of "greedily" in the objectives.

It's very important to emphasize that. I see that as essential.'

'It's got to come across as a product you can't resist. Don't let's forget that we'll pre-test the film before it's broadcast. If our consumer studies aren't conclusive, we bin the film.'

'I'll read back over the objectives. "Eating the product: after opening the pot of Yoplite, the woman eats it irresistibly, with delectation and, obviously, with a spoon."'

'Do you think you're being funny, Octave?'

'Otherwise you might picture the girl walking along with the product in her hand . . .'

'No, no, no! Don't go any further! Yoplite is not an ambulatory yoghurt!'

You make a note of every word they say because it's too true to be beautiful.

'Let's move on to the locations. Gunter, over to you.'

'Vee hef looked at several how-zuz around Mee-amee. Zer are lots off possibilities. Very open or wiz a bick garden, or more modern. Here look ze photo is very terrace-veranda, or vee could alzo do ziss in a traditional farmhowze, ya?'

'But-e,' said Enrique, 'give us your-a recommendatione, Gunter, what is your-a recommendatione?'

'Me, I sink it is good to have ze classic howze wiz ze steps up to ze door. I sink zis is more pretty for you. Vee must not do somesing boring, no?'

'I am-a OK with-a this if you are-a OK.'

'Let's get back to the product shot.'

'It's got to be a yoghurt that has a place in everyday life.

I don't know, have it on the grass to bring out the nature-natural idea.'

'It's a playful product but we've got to milk the health aspect.'

'Ultimately,' Dewler announces eventually, 'what we're aiming for is love. Our customers are buying love.' Now that's going to make Tamara happy, you think to yourself. 'We're not selling yoghurt but mother's milk! That's why we're world-wide. Love is global! We've got to think global! React global! Crap global! Now that's how I see Yoplite's vocation.'

Philip suddenly comes in without knocking. He tells everyone to carry on as if he weren't there, but the meeting goes right back to the beginning all the same, except that this time it's interrupted every now and then by his mobile, which he hasn't switched off.

'She's a woman-woman. She's got unbleached jeans, do you see, a long-sleeved T-shirt, you've got to over-underline the fact that she's relaxed but elegant.'

'It's Sharon Stone only younger and with brown hair.'

'Are you sure that Mrs Cartwright from Orpington is going to recognize herself?'

'Now hang on. She's middle class but fun.'

'She's not very European-looking.'

'Look, we've got nothing against dusky immigrants, it's just our target audience might not identify.'

'She's just a bit Mediterranean. That's the way things are going. Darker complexions are in thanks to the Jennifer Lopez–Inès Sastre–Salma Hayek–Penelope Cruz influence.'

'Who's Salma Hayek?'

'Enrique's seen eighty girls and she's the one who takes the light best.'

'She's exactly right for the image of the product: free, sensuous, one hundred per cent Yoplite.'

'She is-a magnifica.'

'Very cute.'

'Who's Salma Hayek?'

'It's true she communicates with the camera.'

'I'm not against validating this choice once we've viewed the call-back.'

'A peaceful countryside atmosphere but still dynamic. The grass should be green but Mediterranean. Natural sounds, birds singing.'

'We'll have to remember to bring up the crickets at the mixing stage.'

'Who's Salma Hayek?'

'The Latino chick in the druggy Soderbergh film.'

'She's on the cover of Swedish *Vogue* for September.'

'Dunno her.'

The stylist is on the brink of a nervous breakdown. She lays out twenty pairs of sunglasses on the table so the client can choose the ones Tamara should wear. Twenty minutes later, it is finally decided that they should all be taken on the shoot so that the right pair can be chosen *in situ*. (In other words, a decision is made not to make a decision).

'The music. Five musicians have sent demos. Shall we listen to them?'

Demo 1: 'Too hip.'

Demo 2: 'Too hard.'

Demo 3: 'Too kitsch.'

Demo 4: 'Too slow.'

Demo 5: 'Too cheap.'

'Action required,' the producer notes, 'Ask the musicians to rework their demos.'

'I'm against the zoom-in on the tasting shot. I'm afraid it'll distort the girl's body. I'd prefer something more classic in terms of branding.'

That's when Charlie wins his lunch at the Ivy.

'If you find it stress-inducing, we can always play it down.'

The chairman, Philip, stood up at that point and, before leaving the meeting, he turned to the agency's TV producer and said, 'Very good meeting, Martina, well done, very good work. Are you new here? Welcome to The Ross, and I'm pleased with Mark for taking on people like you who've really got your finger on the pulse.'

'Philip, my name's Monica and I've been working here for five years,' replied the TV producer with a coolness that was more than justified.

16

And now you're pretty Yop-lite yourself. You've lost seventeen kilos in three months. You only nourish yourself nasally now. Every morning you wake up with a solid block of chalk up your plastery nose. You get to work at 5.35 in the afternoon. When Mark Browning comments on this, you reply,

'I'm on strike until you fire me.'

'What's the matter? Do you want a raise?'

'No, I'd rather drop everything.'

'Who's been in touch with you? Saatchi's?'

'No, really, I want to stop! Don't you realize I'm dying here? Look how much weight I've lost.'

'Looking like Kate Moss has never been grounds for redundancy.'

'But I'm dying of a brain tumour!'

'Impossible. you haven't got a brain.'

'But my work just doesn't appeal to the general public any more!'

'I know that, but we're not aiming at the general public, we're aiming at the Alpha 1s.'

You're wearing a Canali suit, a shirt by Hedi Slimane for Saint Laurent Rive Gauche-Hommes, Berluti shoes, an

Audemars Piguet Royal Oak watch (until you get your Samsung Watch Phone which will double as a mobile phone), StarckEyes glasses, Banana Republic boxer shorts which you bought in New York. You own your three-bedroom flat in Hoxton Square designed by John Evans. You also own:

- a vertical Bang & Olufsen hi-fi with ten CD players that can be programmed by remote control
- a Cosmo dual-band GSM telephone with integral data-fax
- six William and Mary chairs inherited from your grand-parents
- a Mies van der Rohe Barcelona stool
- a bookcase from the new Fendi interiors collection with a complete set of bound Everyman Classics (unopened)
- a Sony triple-deck video recorder
- the new flat-screen, wall-mounted TV from Philips
- a portable Sony Glasstron DVD
- a 1956 Charles Eames lounge chair
- an Arne Jacobsen Big Brother chair
- a Sony PlayStation 2, Microsoft X-Box and a Nintendo Game Cube
- a pair of Olympus Eye-Trek goggles
- a double-door General Electric fridge (filled with Petrossian caviar, *mi-cuit* foie gras and truffles from La Petite Auberge and Cristal Roederer champagne) with a huge freezer unit and automatic ice-cube maker
- a Sony PC1 digital camcorder (360 grams, 12cm high, 5cm wide)
- an Apple iPod and a Archos Jukebox

- a Leica Digilux Zoom digital camera
- a massive Basquiat and a David Hockney drawing
- a Jean Cocteau poster
- a few originals by Wilhemina Barns-Graham, Euan Uglow, Pierre Le Tan, Edmond Kiraz, Voutch, Mats Gustafson
- and some original sculptures by Vanessa Pooley, Bill Woodrow and Stanley Dove
- an Interdesign coffee table
- three wall recesses, one with a bowl from Corrina Field, one with a vase from Mint and one with a pewter-rimmed fruit bowl by Nic Wood
- an Urban Outfitters standard lamp
- a four-poster bed made from reclaimed chorister stalls originally from a Victorian Gothic church in Hampstead
- eight beige and white pashmina cushions from the Conran Shop
- a framed autograph from Laetitia Casta
- photographic portraits of yourself by Bill Pointer, Jurgen Teller, Liz Collins, David Sims, Rankin
- photographs of yourself with Guy Ritchie, Ridley Scott, Eva Herzigova, Naomi Campbell, Posh and Becks, David Lynch, Jude Law
- a cellar full of premiers grands crus claret delivered by Augé (116 Boulevard Haussmann, Paris): Chasse-Spleen, Lynch Bages, Talbot, Petrus, Haut Brion, Smith Haut Laffitte, Cheval Blanc, Margaux, Latour, Mouton Rothschild . . .
- a thousand CDs, DVDs, CD Roms and video cassettes
- a BMW Z3 in its parking space hired annually from a nearby nightlub

- a lookalike down-and-out outside your front door
- five pairs of loafers from Crockett & Jones, Oliver Sweeney, Patrick Cox, Cesare Paciotti and Emporio Armani
- three pairs of brogues by Johnny Moke, Trickers and Ralph Lauren
- three pairs of Nike Air Max, one pair of Adidas Micropacer (with integrated chronometer and micro-computer to measure the distance covered)
- three Hermès cashmere coats and three Louis Vuitton suede coats
- five suits by Dolce & Gabbana and five by Richard James
- *Sumo*, the huge book of Helmut Newton's photographs published by Taschen (50 x 70cm) on its display stand illustrated by Philip Starck
- five pairs of Helmut Lang jeans and five pairs of Gucci moccasins
- five pairs of trousers from Armand Basi in Conduit Street and five from Krizia
- twenty Prada shirts and five T-shirts each from Muji, Nautica and Boxfresh
- ten Hussein Chalayan eighteen-thread cashmere pull-overs and ten by Lucien Pellat-Finet (you find anything that isn't cashmere is intolerably itchy, except for vicuna)
- a wardrobe holding the Dolce & Gabanna collection in its entirety for the last ten seasons
- a Ruben Alterio painting
- ten pairs of designer sunglasses
- a bathroom kitted out entirely by Calvin Klein (bath towels, bath robes, soap-dish, beauty products,

perfumes, everything except the body lotions which come from Kiehl's in New York)
- the pink iMac on which this book is being written, an orange iBook which can be connected to the Internet without a cable, and an Epson Stylus 740 colour printer.

Most of the other things that you own come from Selfridges. If they don't come from Selfridges then they must come from the Conran Shop. When they're from neither Selfridges nor the Conran Shop, that means you're not at home.

You rarely eat in restaurants for less than £100 a head. When you're travelling, you only ever stay in five-star hotels. It's three years since you've flown anything other than Business Class (otherwise you get a crick-neck when you sleep) with a cashmere blanket (otherwise it itches; see above). For the record, a return flight London–Miami in Business Class costs about £6,000.

With so many belongings and given that you lead such a comfortable life, you should, logically, be happy. Why aren't you? Why do you keep burying your nose in the coke? How can you be unhappy with over a million in your bank account? If you've reached the end of the line, then who's at the other end?

The other day you broke down in tears outside Great Expectations on Wardour Street. In front of little white wooden beds, teddy-bear-shaped bedside lights, pearly grey shoes in 0–3 months size, dungarees for £35, a tiny sweater for £62.50, and you stood there crying like an idiot, and the customers coming out of the shop were horrified, convinced that this poor man sobbing in front of the shop had lost his child in some road accident, but you didn't need an accident to lose your child.

You're going to stuff your face in the cavernous kitchen. You head for the ultra-modern fridge. You can see your reflection in it. You press nervously on the ice-dispenser. Your glass of Absolut overflows with ice. You keep pressing on the lever until the kitchen floor is completely covered in ice cubes. Then you reprogramme the machine to make crushed ice. You start pressing again. It's raining on to the black marble. You contemplate your own face reflected by the most expensive fridge in the world. It was easier behaving like an ageing bachelor when you knew there was someone who loved you waiting at home. You're so full of coke that you sniff your vodka up through a straw. You can feel collapse sneaking up on you. You watch your own decline in the mirror: did you know that etymologically 'narcissistic' and 'narcotic' come from the same word? You've emptied the whole store of ice on the ground. You slide down and end up lying on a bed of crushed snow. You're drowning in freezing particles. You could easily go to sleep among these thousands of icebergs. You could sink like an olive in a giant martini. Absolut Titanic. You're floating on an artificial skating rink. Your frozen cheek is stuck to the floor tiles. There's enough to refresh a whole regiment under your body; and you are in fact an army, in full flight, the retreat from Moscow. You suck the floor. You swallow the blood which flows directly from your nose into your throat. You just have time to call an ambulance on your mobile before you pass out.

see you again straight after . . . this

A young man goes into a launderette. He stops in front of an enormous washing machine 2 metres tall. He puts several coins into the slot, then takes a packet of Ariel washing powder out of his pocket, pours some into his hand and sniffs it up into his nose. He shakes his head, as if invigorated by the Ariel powder he has just sniffed. Then he opens the door to the washine machine and climbs right into it, fully clothed. He sits cross-legged inside the drum. When he closes the door again the machine begins its cycle. He's thrown in every direction and showered with hot water. The camera rotates through 360° to show how quickly the drum is turning.

Suddenly the movement stops. From inside the machine the man sees a very sexy young woman in a miniskirt come into the launderette. The young woman comes over to the enormous machine. Seeing the young man inside, she opens the door and smiles at him. He spits out a mouthful of soapy water. She smiles when she sees the packet of Ariel in front of the machine, puts her hands under her miniskirt and takes off her knickers. She then throws them on to the young man inside the drum before reclosing the door and switching the machine on again. The young man drowns, blowing bubbles against the window.

Ariel logo and packshot – signature: 'Ariel Ultra. Ultra clean even in a machine.'

3 He

'Now the time had come when the rich countries, bristling with industry and overrun with shops, had found a new faith, a project worthy of all the trials man had borne for thousands of years: to unite the world into a single massive corporation.'

René-Victor Pilhes,
L'Imprécateur, 1974

17

A billion people live in shanty towns, according to the Red Cross, but that doesn't hinder Octave's appetite. Look at him chewing his fingernails; it's a start. Browning sent him for a month's detox cure at the Priory because the Cottonwood Clinic in Arizona really did seem a bit far to go. Bosses in the advertising world are like doctor-dealers in sports tournaments: they dope their champions for the performance and put them together again when they fall apart. Is that why they call it a retreat, wondered Octave, so they can treat you again, just with different drugs this time.

He walks through the gardens every morning, slaloming between the ancient oak trees and the mentally ill. He reads only authors who have committed suicide: Hemingway, Kawabata, Gary, Seneca, Petronius, Pavese, Crevel, Zweig, Motherlant, Mishima, LaMarkhe-Vadel, and don't let's forget the girls: Sylvia Plath and Virginia Woolf. (Someone who reads only authors who have committed suicide is actually someone who reads a lot.) For a joke, his assistants sent him a packet of McDougalls flour by Parcelforce. His psychiatrist did not appreciate their humour. Charlie e-mailed a video of a girl with one fist up her pussy and one up her arse to his iBook. That got him smiling again. His experimental treatment with BP 897 should remove any craving for cocaine. If all goes well, he'll soon be able to look at a Mastercard without sneezing.

In the dining room he bumps into new illnesses. For example, the man next door to him explains that he has Aidsaphilia (a new sexual perversion).

'I liked to film girls being shagged without a condom by a friend who's got AIDS. Obviously, the girl never knew. Then I would secretly film her when she went to the lab to pick up the results of her test. The bit that made me come was the moment when the girl realized she was HIV-positive. I ejaculated as she opened the envelope. Aidsaphilia, I invented it. If you only knew how good it feels seeing them breaking down in tears as they leave the lab with their little piece of paper saying HIV-positive in their hands. But I stopped because the police took all my tapes. I did some time and then they put me in here. I'm going to die soon anyway. But now I'm fine, now, I'm fine. I'm fine. Now, thing's are fine now I'm fine I'm fine I'm fine I'm fine I'm fine now I'm fine.'

He stalls and dribbles a bit of mashed carrot on his downy chin.

'I've got a pretty weird kind of sexual fixation too,' says Octave, 'I'm a pastophile.'

'Really? what's that then?'

'It's a perversion which consists chiefly in being obsessed with the past, with my ex. But I'm fine, too, I'm absolutely fine now, everything's fine, now absolutely fine, I'm fine, fine, fine.'

Sophie didn't come to visit him. Did she even know he was in hospital? After about three weeks, Octave managed a few laughs as he watched the schizophrenics gesticulating in the garden. They reminded him of the agency.

'Life is made up of trees, manic-depressives and squirrels.'

Yes, you could say that he's better now. He wanks six times a day. (As he thinks about Anastasia enthusiastically licking Larissa's pussy while Larissa drinks his sperm.) Well, OK, then, maybe Octave hasn't completely recovered.

Whatever, it was time he changed. He was far too 1980s with his coke, his black suits, his loads-a-money and his cheap cynicism. Fashion had moved on. You weren't supposed to show off your money or your achievements now but to pretend to be poor and lazy. A low profile was *de rigueur* in the early years of the new century. Professional Stakhanovites did everything they could to look broke and out of work. Gone were the days of the suntanned, shoulder-padded, brash Thatcherites and of ads with Venetian blinds or fans whirling on the ceiling filmed by Ridley Scott. There are fashions in advertising like in everything else: in the 1950s it was puns; in the 1960s it was humour; in the 1970s it was all youngsters; in the 1980s everything was glitzy; in the 1990s, we took a step back from reality. Now you had to wear an ancient pair of Adidas, a torn Gap T-shirt and a cruddy pair of Helmut Lang jeans, and you had to trim your stubble every day to make it look like three days' growth. You had to have greasy hair, sideboards and a woolly hat, you had to sulk like everyone in *Dazed & Confused*, and to sell black-and-white films in which lanky half-naked anorexics played the guitar. (Or in which massive limousines cruised slowly on a greenish background with saturated colours and fat Puerto Ricans playing volleyball in the rain.) The more obscenely rich you were (people's fortunes had acquired three supplementary noughts with the advent of the Internet), the more down-and-out you looked. All the new millionaires were wearing tattered old trainers. In fact Octave had decided that the minute he set foot outside the clinic he would go and take some fashion tips from his lookalike tramp.

'Strange but true: when I was little, the year 2000 seemed like something out of science fiction. I must have grown up, though, because now it's yesterday's news.'

Octave had time to think in the big old nineteenth-century house. It's as if time moves more slowly at the Priory. Octave wanders round the lawn and picks up a 2,000-year-old pebble. Unlike tubes of toothpaste, pebbles never die. He throws it as far as he can, over by the trees; it will still be there now, as you read these lines. That pebble could spend the next 2,000 years in the same place. That's the way it is: Octave feels jealous of a stone.

He jots down a short verse:

> Give me your hair so lustrous
> Your body so vigorous
> Your eyes so mischievous
> Their blue so rigorous

But, given that he doesn't have anyone to whom he could address it, he offers it to his Aidsaphiliac friend before leaving the clinic.

'Send it to one of your victims. You never know, it might give you a thrill watching a woman's reaction to something other than an HIV-positive result.'

'Let's have a look . . . oh no, are you mad, no, no, that's a serial killer's poem, that is.'

18

Octave waited until the seminar in Senegal to make his entrepreneurial comeback. The Ross is like an army: from time to time it needs to go away on leave, to vacate its barracks; they call these periods 'motivational seminars'. What that adds up to is 250 people in coaches heading for the airport. Lots of married typists (without their husbands), depressive accountants (with their anti-depressants), paternalistic directors, a switchboard operator who used to be a tub of lard but has turned into a beauty since she started shagging the director of human resources on the sly, and a few creative designers making a great effort to laugh so that they look like creative designers. People sing as if they were in a karaoke bar – when they don't know the words, they invent them. Everyone wonders who'll end up sleeping with whom. Octave has high hopes for the local prostitutes, having heard great things about them from Dorothy O'Leary, a friend with the BBC World Service. As for Olivia, eighteen years old, backless top, bandanna in her hair, mules on her feet, denim bag slung over her shoulder, she's sucking on a cola-flavoured lollipop. And 'thinking about life'. How do you know an eighteen-year-old girl? Easy: she has no wrinkles, no bags under her eyes, she has smooth rounded cheeks like a baby, she listens to Robbie Williams on her Walkman and she 'thinks about life'.

Olivia was taken on as a trainee copywriter in Octave's absence. All she really wants is money and fame, but she pretends to be naïve. All the new girls do that: stand there with their mouths half open and great goggling eyes, like Twiggy; the height of ruthless ambition at the moment is to feign innocence. Olivia is telling Octave how she went off to have her tongue pierced all on her own one Saturday afternoon.

'No, it isn't anaesthetized at all, all he does is pull your tongue out using a pair of pincers so that he can drive the bolt through it. But it really doesn't hurt, it's just a bit difficult eating. Well, at first anyway, especially because mine got infected, so everything I ate ended up tasting of pus.'

She keeps her sunglasses on ('They're prescription lenses') and reads only magazines with absurd names (*Talk, Bust, Surface, Nylon, Sleazenation, Soda, Very, Line, Frieze, Crac, Another Magazine*). She sits down next to Octave and when she takes her Walkman off it's only to tell him that she never watches television any more, 'except for *Eurotrash* every now and then'. Octave wonders what the hell he's doing there (same old question, ever since the day he was born). Olivia points out a tower block painfully close to the motorway.

'Look, that's where I live. It's a new development next to a massive football stadium. With the floodlights on at night it's beautiful, it's like living on a film set.'

As Octave doesn't show any interest, she takes the

opportunity to compare hair-removal techniques with a colleague.

'I went to the beauty salon this morning. Laser hair-removal, it really hurts, specially the bikini area. Still, I'm glad it's done for life.'

'Will you remind me to get some Immac at the airport.'

'What time do we get to Dakar?'

'About midnight. I'm going clubbing straightaway. We're only there three nights. Gotta make the most of it.'

'Shit, I forgot my Britney tape!'

'I don't want to get dehydrated in the plane. I always take off my make-up, give myself a facial scrub and then bung on the moisturizer.'

'I do my nails. While my toenails are drying I do my fingernails.'

Octave tries to concentrate his mind. He's got to hang on without his coke, to accept reality in its normal state, to become part of society, respect others, play the game. He wants his return to the outside world to be auspicious not suspicious. That's why he lobs in this opening gambit.

'So, girls, how d'you fancy a quickie with me, then?'

'Sad git.'

'I'd rather die.'

He smiles.

'You're wrong to say no. Girls usually leave it till too late to say yes, when the men have given up, or too soon, when they haven't even been asked yet.'

Stunned silence.

'And, anyway, I'd be prepared to throw in £500.'

'What? He's treating us like whores!'

'Have you looked in the mirror recently? Not even for £5,000.'

Octave laughs a little too loudly.

'I can tell you that Casanova often paid his mistresses. There's nothing wrong in paying for it.'

Then he shows them the ultrasound picture which was posted to him.

'Look at my future child. Doesn't that suddenly make me mega-endearing?'

But he gets the rejection he deserves. The film set is receding in the rear-view mirror. Octave can't even pull any more. He doesn't believe in it enough. If there's one thing that is completely incompatible with irony, it's seduction.

'You wouldn't have an interior-decorating magazine, would you?' asks one of the girls.

'Which one? *Knave? Playboy? Penthouse?*'

'Ha ha. Still hilarious, aren't you? Poor Octave.'

'You know you're becoming pretty lame. I thought they'd sorted your head out.'

'They obviously haven't finished the job. You're Alzheiming completely.'

Octave lowers his eyes and looks at his feet, squeezed into a pair of violet-coloured shoes (each of them worth the monthly salary of most office cleaners). Then he looks up again and moans out loud.

'That's enough. Has it ever occurred to you young ladies that everyone you can see, every prick driving past in his car, all of them, absolutely every one, is going to die, with no exceptions? Him over there in his Audi Quattro. And her, the over-excited forty-something who's just overtaken us in her Austin Mini. And everyone who lives in those blocks of flats cowering behind the ineffectual walls that are meant to cut out the noise of the traffic. Have you even imagined the heap of bodies that would make? Since this planet came into existence, 80 billion people have spent time on it. Keep that image in mind. We walk on 80 million dead bodies. Have you ever visualized the extent of the carnage that all this is going to produce, the scale of putrefaction to come? Life is genocide.'

That's it, he's really ruined everyone's day. He's pleased with himself. He drums his fingers on his little green box of Nytol in the pocket of his Mark Jacobs suede jacket. It reassures him, as a cyanide pill would have reassured a spy about to be interrogated by the Nazis some sixty years ago.

19

The flight is full of ad executives. If it crashed, that would be a first step towards victory for sincerity in the world. But life's not like that, planes full of ad execs don't crash. The planes that crash are full of innocent people, lovers gazing into each other's eyes, the benefactors of this world, Otis Redding, Lynyrd Skynyrd, Manchester United, Marcel Dadi and John Kennedy. These bronzed communicators are so supremely confident because they're quite sure that they're safe. They're more frightened of a stock-market crash than a plane crash. Octave smiles to himself as he types that sentence into his iBook. He is important, he is rich, he is frightened – all that is perfectly compatible. He's drinking a vodka and tonic in British Airways first class. ('In First Class 127 you will enjoy total relaxation in our ergonomically designed seats. They incline at an angle of 127°, which is the angle the body naturally assumes at rest. Each seat is equipped with a telephone, an individual video player and a sound-proofing headset, offering you an ideal environment to work or to relax,' says the blurb in the in-flight magazine).

In Club Class the strategic planners are chatting up the art buyers; the deputy director generals are whispering

sweet nothings to the TV producers; an international coordinator is stroking the thigh of the woman who's director
of development. (You can always tell which girls in a company will sleep with a colleague: they're the only ones who
wear sexy clothes.) This orgy helps to 'reinforce the links
among the personnel of the enterprise, and to optimize
internal communication within the human resource'.
Octave was brought up to accept this sort of thing, and,
given that life is a brief spell allotted to us on a pebble spinning endlessly through space, why waste this brief spell
constantly questioning the *organization*? It's better just to
accept the rules of the game.

'We're trained to accept. I'm surfing on an abyss. For
the last time, isn't there anyone here who wants to fuck
me?'

His provocations used to make people smile; now they
just make them embarrassed.

'After everything man has done for him, God could at
least have gone to the trouble of existing, don't you think?'

Alone in a crowd. He keeps looking inquiringly at his
telephone, but it just repeats: 'You have no new messages in
your voice-mail box.'

Octave goes to sleep in front of a Tom Hanks film (more
than an actor: a sleeping draft). He dreams about a shoot in
the Bahamas where he personally inspects – with his fingers
– Vanessa Lorenzo and Heidi Klum's plucked, dripping
pussies. He doesn't grind his teeth any more. He thinks he's
in the clear. He likes to think that he's taken a step back,
he's in the second degree, he's put some distance between
himself and all this. With a discreet sigh, he pollutes his

Levi 501s (from the 'Sad Tropics' range in the autumn-winter 2001 collection).

And the whole Enterprise landed. The Enterprise reclaimed its baggage. The Enterprise got back into coaches. The Enterprise sang Beatles' songs without realizing how pessimistic they were: 'Yesterday, all my troubles seemed so far away/Now it looks as though they're here to stay', and 'Eleanor Rigby, wearing a smile that she keeps in a jar by the door'. Octave suddenly realizes why the spaceship in *Star Trek* is called the *Enterprise*. Rosserys & Crow isn't unlike a spacecraft lost in the interstellar wastes, searching for extraterrestrials. Come to think of it, quite a few of his colleagues have got pointy ears.

Within moments of arriving at the hotel, the Enterprise disperses. Some of the producers throw themselves into the swimming pool, others throw themselves at the commercial directors, the rest go off to bed. Those who don't feel tired go to the *Roll's* to dance with Olivia and all her breasts. Octave follows them, orders a bottle of Gordon's and has a toke on someone's joint. Things become clearer down on the beach. The black girls haven't let him down.

One of them asks him, 'Feeling hot? Will you come up to my room?'

But with her accent it sounds like, 'Widdecombe?'

Now Octave's fantasies revolve around threesomes, but that wasn't quite what he has in mind. He puts his hand on her face and whispers, 'Sweetheart, I don't fuck girls. I prefer losing them.'

The Saly complex, which is officiously protected by the Senegalese army, comprises fifteen hotels. The agency has favoured the Savana Beach Resort, which boasts not only air-conditioned bedrooms but two swimming pools, which are floodlit at night, tennis courts, mini-golf, a shopping arcade, a casino and a disco, all overlooking the Atlantic Ocean. Africa has changed since Hemingway's safaris. Now it's mainly a continent that the Western world is leaving to die (AIDS killed 2 million people in 1998. The high price charged for the vaccines didn't help). An ideal place to remotivate the average employee. In a land ravaged by the AIDS virus and corruption, amid absurd wars and recurring genocide, this little troop of capitalist personnel regain confidence in the system which keeps it alive. They buy themselves local ebony masks, they manufacture some memories for themselves, kid themselves that they're exchanging views with the locals and send sunny postcards to their families stuck in an English winter to make them jealous. These admen are being shown Africa as a counter-example, so that they can't wait to get home, relieved to confirm that things are even worse somewhere else. Africa acts as an anti-show home. If the poor are dying, no wonder we're so desperate to get rich quick.

They ply through the waves on jet skis, they take Polaroids, no one's interested in anyone, everyone's wearing thongs. In Africa if a white man speaks to a black man, he no longer seems patronizing or condescending, like the colonizers of the past; it's far worse than that now. For now, the white man looks on the black man with the pitying gaze of a priest administering the last rights to someone on death row.

20

Snatches of dialogue from around the pool at the Savana Beach Resort.

One of the directors' assistants (shaking herself): 'Oh, this is lovely!'

Octave: 'So are you.'

A commercial coordinator (as she bites into a mango): 'God, that's so juicy!'

Octave: 'So are you.'

A junior artistic director (making her way to the cafeteria): 'Shall we go and eat?'

Octave: 'Eat who?'

Motivation settles into a full-time routine. The mornings are taken up with self-satisfied meetings in which the company's annual turnover is paraded before the half-naked employees. The terms 'self-financing' and 'long-term investment' come up frequently to justify the absence of end-of-year bonuses. (In fact, all the money earned by this subsidiary is eventually laid at the feet of a few balding old men in Wall Street who never set foot in England, smoke their cigars and don't even say thank you. Like medieval vassals or the victims of the Punic Wars, the directors of

R & C London lay their booty before the shareholders in fear and trembling for the money they owe on their second homes.)

The afternoons are spent in sessions of constructive self-criticism, exploring ways in which the productivity of marketing can be improved. Octave got a nasty case of Montezuma's revenge by putting too much ice in his gin and tonic. Philip the chairman and Mark Browning take him aside from time to time for a quick 'We're very glad you've sorted yourself out, we don't talk about it but we still smile (a bit anxiously) over your little escapades. We may be your bosses but we're very with it, very cool, so don't resign, OK?' None of which stops Philip reminding Octave how crucial the success of the Yoplite shoot is to the agency's relationship with Damione.

'We've just had a Strategic Advertising Committee with them and they gave us a hell of a hard time.'

'Don't worry, Mr Chairman, next time I won't be sick all over the client. And, anyway, did you know I'd found the perfect girl for the film?'

'Yes, I know, the half-caste girl . . . You'll have to touch her up for me in post-production.'

'I'd love to touch her up for you. Don't worry about a thing. It's all budgeted for. You've no idea what they can do nowadays. You can take a girl with a nice arse and overlay another girl's face, a third girl's legs, the hands of a fourth and the tits of a fifth. You can make human patchworks. We're people jockeys!'

'Perhaps you should use a cosmetic surgeon instead of a director to make the film.'

Octave no longer tries to reject everything, but he doesn't want to demean himself either; you could say he's matured. Suddenly he's inflamed by the subject.

'And exactly why can't we use a half-caste for the role? Stop being such a Nazi, you're almost as bad as the client! Christ, I'm fed up with this bloody fascist attitude! Nike ended up looking like they were gunning for the National Front with their Nikepark posters, Nestlé refused to use black people in a basketball sequence. That doesn't mean we have to do the same thing! I mean, where will we end up, if no-one's going to say anything? Advertising's actually becoming revisionist. Gandhi's selling Apple computers! Don't you see? A saintly man who rejected any kind of technology, dressed like a monk and walked barefoot, look at him now, he's been turned into a computer salesman! And Picasso's name has been written all over some new Citroën, Steve McQueen drives a Ford, Audrey Hepburn wears Tod's moccasins! Don't you think they're turning in their graves, poor things, seeing themselves transformed into posthumous sales reps? It's the night of the living dead! Cannibal Holocaust! We're eating corpses! Zombies sell! But how far's this going to go? The Lottery have even brought out posters for a scratch-card with Mao, Castro and Stalin on it! Who's going to say enough is enough if you – Philip, the boss – don't stand up to the racism and denial in global communications?'

'Oh, God, you're such a pain since you stopped snorting all that coke! Do you really think I never think things through? Of course this job makes me want to puke, only I'm thinking about my wife and kids. And I'm not such a megalomaniac that I think I can change everything. For Chrissake, Octave, you should start realizing your limits! All you have to do is switch off the TV and stop going to McDonald's. This shit everywhere isn't my fault, it's yours, you who buy the Nikes made by the Indonesian slaves! It's easy to whinge about the system and support it at the same time! And, anyway, stop treating me like an idiot under the pretext that I'm loaded with money! Obviously there are things I can't stand. Not so much the fact that we have to cast white people, because there's not much we can do about that. It's the target audience who are racists not the advertisers. Nor do I mind the trick with the talking corpses. The public have never really understood the great artists. All those poor geniuses were turning in their graves before they were even dead. No, what annoys me, my little Gucche, is all these new celebrations that advertising has invented to push people into buying things. I'm fed up with watching my family walking right into their traps. I mean, Christmas, fine (even if Father Christmas was invented by some American distribution chain), but Easter Day's sponsored by Thorntons, there's Mother's Day, Father's Day, Halloween, Bonfire Night, St Patrick's Day, St Valentine's Day, Thanksgiving, which Bernard Matthews will latch on to any minute, the Chinese New Year, the Russian New Year, Nutrasweet Day, Tupperware parties! Whatever next? Soon the whole calendar will be filled up with brand names. There won't be saints' days any more, just 365 different logos!'

'Well, there you are then, boss, I was right to corner you on that one. I hate Halloween too. It used to be All Saints'

Day, I don't see why we had to go and import some trans-atlantic celebration.'

'Ah, but that's because it's exactly the opposite! On All Saints' Day people used to go and visit the graves of the dead, but with Halloween it's the dead who come and visit us. It's much more practical. No one has to lift a finger. It's all on our doorsteps: DEATH COMES KNOCKING ON THE DOOR! That's what they love about it! Death the travelling salesman, like a postman coming to flog you the post office's official calendar!'

'I think what it boils down to is people would much rather dress up as ghosts and ghouls and stick a candle in a pumpkin than think about the loved ones they've lost. But you missed the most important commercial celebration out of your list, Philip. Marriage. Marriage fuels the most intensive advertising and promotional campaigns every year, as soon as we're into January. It starts with the posters for Pronuptia, then the wedding lists at Harrods and Debenhams. It's on the cover of all the women's magazines, it overdoses on radio and TV. Young couples are completely brainwashed. They think they're getting married because they love each other and they're going to be happy together, but it's just because someone wants to sell them a dinner service, a set of bath towels, a coffee-maker, a sofa, a microwave . . .'

'Hey, that reminds me of something . . . Octave, do you remember on the Zanussi account you suggested a baseline with the word "happiness" in it?'

'Oh yes . . . The legal department said we couldn't use it or something, didn't they?'

'Yes! Because the word "happiness" has been branded by Nestlé! *Happiness belongs to Nestlé.*'

'Well, that doesn't surprise me at all. Did you know Pepsi want to register blue as a trademark?'

'What?'

'Yup, absolutely true, they want to buy the colour blue, to own it. And that's not all. They finance educational CD Roms which are distributed free in primary schools. So children are doing their lessons in school on Pepsi computers. They learn to read the word "thirsty" next to the "Pepsi" colour.'

'And when they look up at the Pepsi sky, their Pepsi eyes light up, and if they fall off their bikes they get Pepsi-coloured bruises all over their knees . . .'

'It's the same with Colgate. They're offering video tapes to teachers to explain to children that they should brush their teeth with toothpaste.'

'Yes, I've heard about that. L'Oréal are doing the same thing with their "kids'" shampoo. Washing their brains wasn't enough for them, they want to wash their hair as well!'

Philip bursts into a rather excessive laugh . . . This doesn't stop Octave from going on.

'I find it very reassuring that you're interested in all this.'

'It's quite clear to me. So long as there's nothing else there, advertising will take up all the available space. It's become the only ideal. It's not nature that abhors a vacuum, it's hope.'

'That's terrible. No, hang on, don't go. Now that we're

actually talking to each other, I've got an even better anecdote. When the advertisers can't think of new ways of selling things, or just for the sake of it, to justify their indecent salaries, they decide they need to *change the packaging*. Then they pay a fortune to some design company to give their product a new look. They have endless meetings. I was at Kraft Jacobs Suchard once with some guy with a crew cut called Tony Piddle, or Puddle, or Paddle – something like that . . .'

'Peddle.'

'Yes, that's it, Peddle – you don't forget that in a hurry in this line of business. He was showing me the various logos he had to choose from. He wanted my opinion. He was ecstatic, practically having an orgasm. He felt useful and important. He laid all the packaging mock-ups on the ground in his natty designer office block, him with his close-cropped hair and his Wallace and Gromit tie, me on a downer and needing another line, and we drank coffee that some ageing, wheezing secretary who hadn't been fucked for thirty years brought us. I looked him right in the eye and I felt that at that moment he was beginning to wonder. For the first time in his life he was asking himself what the hell he was doing there. And I told him it didn't matter which one he chose and he ended up picking the most sober contender at random by saying, "Ip, dip, sky blue, who's it, not you!" And that pack now sits on the shelves of every supermarket all over Europe . . . Isn't that the most amazing parable? *Our conditioning was chosen at random.*'

But Philip had turned on his heel and left some time ago. He doesn't like being persuaded to bite the hand that feeds him. He avoids any prolonged confrontation. His only act of revolt is limited to a 'monthly bout of self-mockery to earn a nice lunch at the Oxo Tower'. That's why he feels tired a little earlier every day.

Octave breathes the hot air in and out. Sailing boats glide silently across the bay. All the girls from the agency are having their hair braided because they want to look like Iman Bowie (result: they look like Bo Derek, only old). On the Day of Judgement, when everyone in advertising is asked to account for themselves, Octave will be held only partially responsible. He will have been only an appa-ratchik, a rather weak employee, who even, at some point, had his doubts – his stay at the Priory would probably provide him with mitigating circumstances and make the jury more lenient in his case. Apart from anything else, unlike Browning, he's never won a Lion at Cannes.

He rings Tamara, his platonic prostitute, while he thinks about Sophie, the mother of the child he'll never see. Too many absentee women in his life.

'Did I wake you?'

'I had a client at the Plaza last night,' she croaks. 'Can't tell you, his dick was like a baby's arm. I needed a bloody shoe-horn to get him up my pussy. WHISKAS – SEVEN OUT OF TEN OWNERS WHO EXPRESSED A PREFERENCE SAID THEIR CATS PREFERRED IT.'

'What the hell was that?'

'That? Oh, nothing, it's so I don't have to pay for the phone. They put ads on every now and then and I get the call for free.'

'I can't believe you signed up for that!'

'JEWSONS. WE'VE GOT THE JEWSON LOT. Yup, well, you can live with it, you'll see. I've got used to it. Anyway, this customer last night, luckily he was completely pissed, he was only half up, but hung like a donkey, I swear to you. So, anyway, I did a little striptease for him on the bed, he asked if he could sniff a gee off my foot, and afterwards we watched TV. I think I coped pretty well. SAINSBURY'S – MAKING LIFE BETTER. What's the time?'

'Three o'clock in the afternoon.'

'Ohhh, my God, I'm knackered. I was dead on my feet at the Banana at seven this morning, with my false eyelashes stuck to my teeth. What about you, are you OK? Where are you?'

'In Senegal. I miss you. I'm just reading a book about prostitutes.'

'Stop mucking about. I'm going to puke up in my handbag. MR KIPLING MAKES EXCEEDINGLY GOOD CAKES. Can't you call me back later?'

'Have you got the mobile next to your ear? You should be careful. Cellular phones mess up your DNA. They've done tests on mice. Their mortality rate goes up seventy-five per cent if they're exposed to mobile phones. I've bought an earpiece to plug into mine. You should get one. *I* don't want a brain tumour.'

'But, Octave, you haven't got a brain. BARCARDI BREEZER – THERE'S LATIN SPIRIT IN EVERYONE.'

'Look, I'm sorry, but I've got a problem with your jingles. I'm hanging up. Go back to sleep, my gazelle, my Berber beauty.'

*

The problem with modern man isn't that he's evil. Quite the opposite. In general, for practical reasons, he prefers to be nice. It's just he hates being bored. Boredom terrifies him, when, in fact, there is nothing more constructive and generous than a good daily dose of dead time, moments of soul-destroying tedium and mind-boggling dreariness, alone or collectively. Octave has grasped this: true hedonism is actually boredom. Boredom alone allows us to enjoy each moment on its own merits, but everyone tries to persuade us otherwise. To alleviate their boredom, Westerners escape through various intermediaries – television, cinema, the Internet, the telephone, video games or even just magazines. They're never actually doing what they're doing, they only ever live by proxy, as if there were something wrong in being happy just to breathe, here and now. When you're in front of the TV or an interactive website, or when you're speaking to someone on your mobile, or playing on your PlayStation, you're not living. You are somewhere else, not in the place you're in. You may not be dead, but you're not very much alive either. It would be interesting to measure how many hours a day we spend like this, somewhere that isn't where and when we actually are. All these machines will end up listing us as absent or uncontactable, and it's going to be very difficult to get back out. Everyone who criticizes showbiz society has a TV at home. Everyone who's contemptuous about our consumer society has a Visa card. There's no getting out. Nothing has changed since Pascal's days: man is still trying to run away from his fears by distracting himself. It's just that now the distractions have become so ubiquitous that they've taken

God's place. How do you escape from distraction? By confronting your fears.

The world isn't real, except when it's boring.

Octave takes delight in being bored to tears under a coconut tree. His happiness rests on the fact that he's just sitting there watching two grasshoppers mating on the sand while he mumbles.

'The day everyone agrees to be bored here on Earth, humanity will be saved.'

His delicate state of tedium is interrupted by a grumpy Mark Browning.

'So, is it really all over with Sophie?'

'Yup. Well, I dunno . . . Why're you asking me that?'

'Oh, nothing. Can I have a quick word?'

'Even if I said no, you'd still talk to me, and I'd be forced to listen to you for hierarchical reasons.'

'You're right. So shut up, then. I've seen the storyboard you sold for Yoplite. It's disastrous. How the hell did you hatch out a load of shit like that?'

Octave rubs his ear to check that he heard right.

'Hang on, Mark, *you* were the one who said we should drop a cowpat on that job!'

'Me? I never said any such thing.'

'Have you lost your memory or something? We had twelve campaigns thrown back in our faces and you said we had to go in with the National Emergency Operation, the Last-minute Cowpat, to . . .'

'Sorry to interrupt but you're the sick druggie who's just come out of a clinic, so don't try and switch roles, OK? I know what I tell my creative team. I would never have let you show a piece of shit like that to one of the agency's showcase clients. I'm fed up crapping with shame every time I go out to dinner. "YOPLITE. KEEPS YOU IN SHAPE, MIND AND BODY." I mean, really, who are you trying to kid?'

'Hang on, Mark. I might just accept that you're lying about what happened, that's normal. But the Yoplite script's been sold now, it tested well, we've already had two pre-production meetings. It's a bit late to change everything. I've thought about this a lot and—'

'I didn't hire you to think. You can never hide from the possibility of finding a better campaign. Until the film is actually on the air, everything can be changed. So I'm telling you something. You and Charlie are going to find a way of changing this script during the shoot. For Chrissake, the whole image of The Ross is at stake!'

Octave nods and shuts his mouth. He knows perfectly well that it's not the image of The Ross which is pre-occupying his art director, but the fact that his swanky office chair is in the process of becoming an ejector seat. Philip must have come and whispered in his ear about it beforehand, and that means maximum pressure must have been brought to bear by Damione. This whole story smells of musical chairs. Put another way: there's redundancy in the air this evening in Senegal. Someone is about to be told, 'You are the weakest link, goodbye.' And, unfortunately, Octave feels intuitively that it won't be him.

21

On the second evening the master of ceremonies had organized an outing into the bush. The aim: to make the long-term employees believe that they were going to see a bit of open country, to escape from their luxury prison. But, obviously, nothing of the sort actually happened. They were transported by four-wheel drive to the edge of Lake Rose to watch African dancing and to eat a traditional *mechoui*, but they wouldn't see anything real. They were only making the trip so that they could confirm that the scenery looked like the brochure provided by the tour operator. Tourism turns every traveller into a quality-control inspector, discovering by verifying, being dazzled simply by locating the dazzling; the backpacker as a sort of doubting Thomas. Mind you, Octave was being eaten alive by the mosquitoes; it was still possible to experience an element of adventure if you'd left your citronella spray in your hotel bedroom.

After the supper, a Senegalese wrestling competition was organized between the seminarists (all Lacoste-branded) and the fake tribal warriors (dressed up as natives from a Tarzan film). This afforded an opportunity to admire Browning in his Y-fronts rolling in the mud, to a background of tom-

toms, under the giant baobab tree, the moon and the stars, with petrol-flavoured wine, the toothy laugh of the director of external relations, the famished eyes of the local children, the powerful Casamance pot and the spicy food making Octave feel once again that he wanted to hug the sky and thank the universe for being here – if only provisionally.

He liked the permanent humidity which made hands slide suavely over skin. It gave every kiss a fiery urgency. Every detail takes on extra importance when nothing makes sense any more. The least that an addict had to do was to kick the habit. Octave had come on this compulsory trip only reluctantly; and now here he was contemplating the sublime, grappling with eternity, embracing life, overcoming absurdity and understanding simplicity. When the dealer known as Goldmine delivered his daily supply of weed, he prostrated himself on the beach mumbling 'Sophie', a name that winded him just to think of it.

'Love hasn't got anything to do with the heart, the heart's a disgusting organ, a sort of pump full of blood. Love is primarily concerned with the lungs. People shouldn't say, "She's broken my heart" but "She's stifled my lungs." Lungs are the most romantic organs: lovers and artists always contract tuberculosis. It's not coincidence that Chekhov, Kafka, D. H. Lawrence, Chopin, George Orwell and St Thérèse of Lisieux all died of it; as for Camus, Moravia, Boudard and Katherine Mansfield, would they have written the same books if it weren't for TB? Besides, as far as we know, the Lady of the Camellias didn't die of a heart attack; that's a punishment reserved for stressed-out wannabes, not the sentimental and the lovesick.'

Octave was flying and talking to himself.

'Everyone's got some heartache slumbering in their depths. Any heart that hasn't been broken isn't a heart at all. Lungs have to wait until they've got tuberculosis to know that they exist. I am your instructor on the subject of consumption. You have to have a shadow in your ribcage, like Little Nell in *The Old Curiosity Shop* or Mme Chauchat in *The Magic Mountain*. I liked to watch you sleeping, even when you were only pretending. When I came home late, drunk, I used to count your eyelashes. Sometimes it looked to me as if you were smiling at me. A man in love is a man who likes to watch his wife sleeping, and, from time to time, having an orgasm. Sophie, can you hear me all those hundreds of miles away, like in that Nokia ad? Why do people have to go away before we realize we loved them? Can't you see that all I wanted was to have a slight pulmonary embolism, like in the early days?'

But the topless typists had turned up, and Olivia, the busty trainee. They were handing round a phallic-shaped pipe of grass, giving rise to a series of smutty jokes.

'Nothing like sharing it around.'

'I keep sucking but nothing's coming out.'

'Are you sure you're taking it in properly.'

'We'll go round again, but you'll have to wash it first.'

It seems a bit vulgar on paper but in context it was hilarious.

Their managerial colleagues of the male sex all had sweaters over their shoulders, knotted carelessly and slung over their pink Ralph Lauren polo shirts. Octave found this unacceptable and flew off the handle.

'*What the hell's the matter with them all, with their sweaters tied over their shoulders!* It's either one thing or the other. Either it's cold and you put your sweater on, or it's hot and you leave it at home. Wearing your sweater over your shoulders shows weakness, spinelessness, an inability to make decisions, a fear of draughts, a lack of foresight, and a pathetic desire to show off your Shetland (because, obviously, these gentlemen are too tight to buy themselves cashmere). They wear this sort of limp octopus round their necks because they can't even choose an outfit to suit the weather. Anyone who wears a sweater on their shoulders is chicken, ugly, impotent and weak. Girls, please swear to me that you'll avoid them like the plague. *Say no to the tyranny of sweaters over the shoulders!*'

Then it was the night, and then the day, and barbecued lobster. Who mentioned decolonization? There's nothing like global advertising for colonization: in the furthest corner of the smallest hut on the ends of the earth, Nike, Coca-Cola, Gap and Calvin Klein have replaced England, France, Spain and Belgium. Only the little black children have to make do with crumbs from the table: imitation baseball caps, fake Rolexes and Lacoste shirts with a counterfeit crocodile which falls off the first time you wash it. The rosé's a bit rough, but that's what it's there for, isn't it? They get through seventeen bottles between eight of them. Charlie's high as a kite – throwing himself idiotically into all the activities laid on by the hotel, the conga, karaoke contests, wet T-shirt competitions, and he hands out McDonald's toys to all the native children, who clamour for them, saying '*Cadeau! Cadeau!*'

Octave knows that this lie will come to an end first thing on Monday morning. But when a lie stops that doesn't necessarily mean you go back to reality. It's all a pack of lies, each lying on top of the next. 'Lies are the mortar that bind the savage individual man into the social masonry.'

God, it's all so complicated, if you don't watch out, it need only take one to catch you out.

Charlie slaps Octave on the back and Octave hands him his joint.

'Hey, did you know Pepsi wanted to register blue as a trademark?'

'Yeah, 'course I knew that, Charlie, and happiness belongs to Nestlé. What do you take me for? I know what's going on in the news . . .'

'Exactly. Look at this.' Charlie brandishes a copy of *The Times*. 'I've got something even better for your book. The Institute of Media Statistics has just perfected a new system for measuring audience figures. It's a little box which contains an infra-red camera to monitor eye movement, and a watch with a microphone, a micro-processor and a memory to record what the ears are doing. They're finally going to know what consumers are looking at and listening to in the home, but not just on TV, in their cars, at the supermarket, everywhere! *Big Brother is watching you!*'

Charlie drags on the joint and starts coughing. Octave nearly dies laughing.

'Go on, cough, Mr Last Bastion of Hope, cough away.

It's the best thing for it. It's just as well Orwell got TB, after all. He didn't have to stay around to see how right he was.'

The motivational seminar begins in collectivist utopia. Suddenly we're all equals, the slaves feel totally at ease with their bosses, giving rise to a sort of social orgy. For the first evening at least. Because the very next day the clan resumes its original structure, and there's no mixing except at night, in the corridors, where people exchange room keys. This farce then becomes the only form of utopia. One of the women from the legal department, pissed as a fart, is squatting to pee in the garden; one secretary is having lunch on her own because no one wants to eat with her; an artistic director on tranquillizers gets aggressive as soon as she's had a bit much to drink (really violent: slapping people, punching them in the eye, she even tore Octave's shirt); in fact there isn't a single normal person on this trip. Life within the company engenders a sort of schoolboy cruelty, only more violent, because there's no one there to protect you. Unacceptable jibes, unjustified attacks, sexual harassment and power struggles: anything goes. It's like your worst memories of the school playground. The affected relaxed atmosphere of the advertising world re-creates the school nightmare to the power of a thousand. Everyone is crude and unkind to everyone else, as if they were eight years old, and you have to take it all with a smile, on pain of being thought 'uncool'. It goes without saying that the sickest individuals are the ones who think they're the most normal: deputy director generals convinced that it's their God-given right to be deputy director generals; account directors sure that they should really be chairman; commercial managers waiting for their retirement; bosses in the hot seat; director generals on the gravy train. But where the hell's Jeff? Octave hasn't seen him the whole trip. Shame, he's usually well up on what's going down. He would know what was making all the directors of The Ross so nervous. Dewler-is-a-shit must have stabbed them all in the back again.

On the beach Octave is moved to tears at the sight of sand stuck to the girls' skin by their sweat, of the bruises on their thighs, the grazes on their knees. One more drag and he'd be ready to fall in love with a shoulder blade. He needs his daily ration of beauty spots. He kisses Olivia's arm because she's wearing Obsession. He talks to her about her elbow for hours.

'I love your elbow, the way it points towards the future. Let me look at it, let me admire it. You have no idea of the power it has. I like your elbow more than I like you yourself. Go on, light your cigarette, bring the flame up to your face. Try to distract me if you like, you won't stop me kissing your elbow. Your elbow is my life-belt. Your elbow's saved my life. Your elbow exists, I've met it. I bequeath my body to your elbow, so fragile it makes me want to weep. Your elbow is made up of bone with skin over the top. The skin is slightly worn. As a child you made it bleed. In those days there was quite often a scab here, where I'm kissing now. An elbow isn't much and yet, try as I might, I can't think of another reason to be alive at this precise moment.'

'You're so sweet.'

'All I want right now is to lick your elbow. Then I can die.'

He recites:

> 'Your elbow is, my sweet Olivia,
> As nice as white powder from Bolivia.'

Then, using Olivia's back as a desk, our tanned Valmont writes a postcard to Sophie:

Dear Obsession,

Would you be so kind as to save me from myself? Otherwise I'm going to stand in the water and put my hands in a socket. There's one thing worse than being with you: that's not being with you. Come back. If you come back I'll give you a new Beetle. No, OK, that's not much of an offer, but it's your fault. Since you left I'm becoming more and more serious. I've realized that there isn't anyone else like you. So I've concluded that I must be in love with you.

No point in signing it, Sophie would recognize such a distinctive style. Just after sending the postcard, Octave regretted not begging her on his knees: 'Help, I can't go on. I can't get by without you, Sophie. I just can't believe we're not together. If I lose you I lose everything.' Shit, that's what he should have been doing, grovelling at her feet. Couldn't he even do that?

Before Sophie he used to chat girls up by giving them a hard time for having false eyelashes. In those days he used to ask them to close their eyes so that he could check, and he would grab the opportunity to kiss their dazzling lips. He also had the lorry trick.

'Say "lorry".'

'Lorry.'

'Beep, beep!' (touching their breasts).

And don't let's forget the bet.

'I bet I can touch your arse without touching your clothes.'

'OK.'

'Oh, I've lost!' (putting his hand on their arse).

And then there was the 'Tequila boom boom' trick. You ask a girl to hold a slice of lime between her teeth, you put salt on her neck, you lick up the salt, down a shot of Tequila with lemonade in one, and then bite the slice of lime from her mouth. After three rounds like that, a tongue is usually substituted for the lime.

Contrary to all expectations, these strategies actually worked. With Sophie it was different. He led her to believe that he was really interested in her and what she had to say. And she pretended to listen to him. They ended up believing what they didn't say. And then one day she asked him, 'Why do you never say anything?'

'It's a very good sign when I don't say anything: it means I'm intimidated. It's a very good sign when I'm intimidated: it means something's got to me. It's a very good sign when something's got to me: it means I'm falling in love. And when I fall in love . . . that's a very bad sign.'

He loved her because she was married. He fell in love with her because she wasn't free. He was working with her at the time but he couldn't have her. He also loved her because he was married and it was forbidden, secret and the wrong thing to do. He loved her like every woman he wasn't allowed to flirt with: his mother, his sister, his father's girlfriends, and his first love, an impossible, unrequited love. Love is like a game of dominoes: the first time you fall in love triggers all the subsequent falls. He wanted her like all the pretty girls he'd admired as a child, without them even knowing it. He told her, 'When I fall in love that's a very bad sign', and that didn't surprise her at all. He arranged to meet her on Waterloo Bridge, just at a turn in the river, so the Thames looked like a pair of arms embracing the future. Afterwards, it all became almost too lovely to be true. All it needed was for her to be there.

'Excuse me, I wonder whether I could have your telephone number, should I wish to get in touch with you another time?'

'Well, of course, sir.'

'Octave, please call me Octave. I think that I'm in love with you. I do hope it won't disturb you if I unleash myself upon your breasts, Madam?'

'Please, make yourself at home. But perhaps you would consider turning your tongue around inside my mouth seven times before you speak again?'

'Do you have some premises to which we could repair?'

It's a shame to fall in love so easily. An explosion of sensuality waits just round the corner for people when they get it together. Pleasure is like a sword of Damocles hanging over marriage. Sophie took him to the agency's car park under Carlisle Street, a dark, quiet place where they made love against a concrete pillar, standing between two company cars. The longest orgasm either of them had ever had. Afterwards she borrowed his mobile phone, keyed in her number and put it into the memory.

'There, now you won't be able to say you've lost it!'

Octave was so in love with her that his body rebelled the moment they were apart. He developed spots, allergic reactions, great red patches on his neck, stomach cramps and constant insomnia. When the brain thinks it controls everything, the heart revolts and the lungs empty themselves. Anyone who denies their love becomes a real sight and gets ill. Being without Sophie was making Octave ugly. The same is still true today; it's not just the drugs that he misses.

'My dick's screaming famine!'

Octave yells into the microphone. Olivia undulates. Octave is playing the records in the hotel's nightclub. He has to make do with what there is: a few disco albums, some compilations and three crumbling 45s. He just about manages to keep the dance floor full with the available material, including the most beautiful song in the world: Donna Summer's 'Upside down/Boy, you turn me/Inside out/and round and round.' But he also succumbs to easy crowd pleasers like 'YMCA'.

'The Village People are like wine,' Octave announces, 'they get better with age.'

Anything rather than Buck's Fizz. Every now and then Olivia comes and presses herself up against him in front of her friends. And as soon as her friends move away, she peels herself off him. It's not him that she likes, it's *him in front of her own girl band.* He feels old and ugly in a world where everyone is young and beautiful. He catches hold of her wrist angrily.

'Little prick-teasers of eighteen are a pain, you know.'

'Not as much as thirty-three-year-old divorcés.'

'The only thing that I'll never be able to change about you is my age.'

He chases lots of pretty girls to avoid wondering why he chases lots of pretty girls. He knows the answer only too well: so that he doesn't have to stay with just one.

Later, nothing happened. Octave took Olivia back to her room; she kept stumbling. He lay down on her bed. She slunk off to the bathroom and he heard her being sick. Then she pulled the flush and brushed her teeth, hoping he hadn't noticed. When she took her clothes off, Octave pretended to be asleep, then he really did go to sleep. The room smelt of Colgate-flavoured sick.

On the flight back there was an alarming avalanche of newly blow-dried hair and an equally alarming shortage of deodorant. Octave sang 'Love Story' at the top of his lungs:

> 'Where do I begin
> To tell the story
> Of how great a love can be,
> The sweet love story
> That is older than the sea,
> Where do I start?
> With your first hello
> You gave a meaning to this empty world of mine,
> There'll never be another love another time,
> You came into my life and made the living fine,

You fill my heart.'

Strange how something you think about only super-ficially suddenly takes on so much meaning.

'You fill my soul with wild imaginings.'

No one of his generation dares to talk like that any more.

'You fill my heart with so much love
that everywhere I go I'm never lonely.'

He'd cried with laughter at those words so often. Why did he find them so ridiculous? Why does anything romantic make us feel so uncomfortable? We're ashamed of our emotions. Pathos is hunted out like the plague. We're not going to gain anything by cultivating this hard attitude.

'How long can it last,
Can love be measured by the hours in a day?
I have no answers now but this much I can say;
I know I'll need you till the stars all burn away . . .'

The secretaries are giggling now but they would dissolve into tears at the first man who looked them in the eye and said, 'I know I'll need you till the stars all burn away.' Maybe they're sniggering nervously with envy. They change the subject, talk about the reduced-rate photo-processing package available on the company. When they talk about the directors, they refer to them only by their initials:
'Has FHP spoken to PJT about this?'

'You'd have to ask JFD.'

'The PPM went well with HPT and RGP.'

'Yes, but LG and AD didn't sanction anything.'

For the rest of the flight they grumble about their non-existent Christmas bonuses. Octave persistently tries to laugh louder than everyone else and, sometimes, he succeeds.

22

After the invisible man, the invincible woman. In a plane
flying in exactly the opposite direction, just a few days
later, Sophie read Octave's postcard and didn't find it amusing. She was carrying his baby but she didn't love him. In
fact, she'd been seeing Mark Browning for a month now,
and was on her way to join him in Senegal, where he was
staying for a short holiday.

At first she'd martyred herself over it. Dumping someone that you love, when you're nurturing their child in
your belly, requires superhuman courage. No, correction,
that should be *sub-human* courage: animal courage. It's a
bit like cutting off your leg with a rusty Stanley knife without anaesthetic, only slower. Then she wanted revenge. Her
love had turned to hate, and that's why she rang Octave's
boss, having worked for him a few years earlier. He'd asked
her out for lunch and that was where she'd snapped,
broken down and poured it all out over the table at Zilli
Fish. Browning had just split up with his latest model, so
that worked out rather nicely in terms of timing. They'd
ordered a pretentious dish of queen scallops. Octave had
rung Sophie on her mobile while Mark's feet were already
making advances under the table.

'Hello, Sophie? Why do you never return my calls?'

'I haven't got your number.'

'What do you mean, you haven't got my number?'

'I erased it from my mobile.'

'But why?'

'It was taking up some of my memory.'

She'd hung up, switched off her phone and then let herself be kissed over her *mi-cuit* chocolate fondant cake. The next day, she changed her number.

Sophie had erased what was taking up some of her memory.

Octave didn't know about her relationship with Mark, but if he had he would have thought himself lucky: to be cuckolded by your employer was equivalent to indirect redundancy. Sophie's flight didn't crash either. Browning was waiting for her at Dakar airport. They made love once a day, for eight days. At their age they were beginning to feel that was a lot. Neither of them was unhappy; they liked lazing around together. Everything suddenly seemed so simple and obvious to them. As you get older you don't get happier, no, you lower your expectations of happiness. You're more tolerant, you say when something's not right, you're serene. Every second of respite is worth having. Mark and Sophie didn't *look* good together but they *felt* good together, which is much more unusual. The only thing that bothered them was that by being together they'd made the initials M & S, a high street giant going down the pan.

But that can't be why they decided to die. Can it?

don't go away! the book continues after the break.

A bearded young dealer is standing above a public waste tip with his arms spread to form a cross. Twelve clients stand round him in a circle. They're wearing hooded sweatshirts, cagoules, baseball caps and baggy shorts. They have come to venerate him in this wasteland.

Suddenly he says, 'verily I say unto you, which man among you will cast the first stone?'

Then one of the apostles hands him a pebble of cocaine. 'Here, O Lord, is a G.'

Sacred music swells as a ray of light from the sky lights up the white pebble, which our sacred dealer brandishes, crying, 'you are the rock, and on this rock shall I build my epilogue.'

Then our bearded superstar crumbles the pebble in his hand to a white powder. When he opens his hand again, there are twelve perfectly parallel lines on the palm of his hand.

'Take ye all of this and sniff it, for this is my soul which is given for you.'

The twelve disciples fall to their knees among the house-hold waste and cry, 'Hallelujah! He has multiplied the lines!'

Packshot: white powder heaped up in the form of a cross with straws stuck in it.

Signature in voice-off: 'Cocaine. To try it once is to try it again and again.'

4 We

'In order to present our message with any chance
of producing a lasting impression on the public,
we have had to kill some people.'

Theodore Kaczynski
a.k.a. 'Unabomber',
manifesto printed in the *Washington Post*
and the *New York Times*, 19 September 1995

23

We were shocked by Mark's suicide. But it would be lying to say that we were surprised by it. The official version says that he drowned off the coast at Saly, carried away by the undertow. But we all know that he let himself be dragged under to escape from the trials of this life. We all knew that Mark was stressed out, we could tell that he was struggling, we relied on his simulated drive and enthusiasm, and we changed the subject when he talked about self-destruction. We ignored the evidence: Browning was killing himself and we had no intention of saving him. We were arranging his funeral before he was even dead. 'The king is nearly dead, long live the king!' At the funeral there were 300 advertising people snivelling in the cemetery, especially those who hated Mark and who'd been wanting him to die for ages. They felt guilty because their prayers had been answered, and they wondered who they could find to hate now. To get ahead in advertising, you have to have an enemy to crush; it's very disconcerting to be suddenly robbed of such a crucial driving force.

We would have preferred it if the service had just been a dream. We were watching an *agent provocateur* being committed to the ground, and, as we watched his coffin being lowered into the dark hole, we all hoped that this was a far-fetched ploy of his. Wouldn't it have been great if the camera had suddenly zoomed out and we'd realized that the whole thing had been organized by actors: the priest would turn out to be a comedian, the tearful friends would burst into laughter, a team of technicians behind us would unwind reels of cable and a director would cry, 'Cut!' But no one cried, 'Cut!'

We often wish our lives were just a dream. We'd like to wake up, like they do in bad films, and be able to resolve all our problems thanks to this subterfuge. As soon as a character drowns in the cinema, hurray, he's brought back to life. How many times have we seen that on the screen: the hero's attacked by a seething, carnivorous monster, he's trapped at the end of a narrow gully, but, just as the terrifying creature is about to devour him, bang, there he is sitting up in bed in a mucky sweat? Why doesn't that happen in real life? Hey?

How exactly do you wake yourself up when you're not sleeping?

There was a coffin with a real body in it. We cried real tears. When I say we, I mean everyone at The Ross London: Jeff, Philip, Charlie, Olivia, the trainees, the powerful, the useless, and me, Octave with his tissue, Octave still there, not fired, not resigned, just a bit disappointed that Sophie didn't come. By 'we' I mean all the parasites maintained by The Ross's money: television magnates, shareholders in major radio companies, singers, actors, photographers, designers, politicians, magazine editors, chairmen of large chain stores, we the deciders, we the opinion-leaders, we the artists who've sold our souls, famous or doomed, we wept. We wept for our pitiful fate. When someone in advertising dies, there aren't any articles in the papers, there aren't any flags at half-mast, there aren't any interrupted television programmes, there are just some unsold stock options and an unused Swiss bank account under a secret number. When someone in advertising dies, he's just replaced by someone in advertising who's alive.

24

A few days later, South Beach, Miami. There are pamela-andersons in every size, and jeanclaudevandammes galore. We're all Friends. We did plenty of UV sessions before baring our faces to the sun. If you want to hold your own in this sort of place you have to look like a bimbo or a porn star. We take drugs because the alcohol and the music alone don't give us the strength to speak. We live in the world in which the only adventure consists of screwing without a condom. Why are we all chasing after beauty? Because this world is so ugly it makes us want to puke. We want to be beautiful because we want to be the best. Cosmetic surgery is the last ideology left. Everyone has the same mouth. The world is appalled by the thought of human cloning when it actually already exists and it's called 'plastic surgery'. In all the bars Cher is singing 'Do you believe in life after love?' From now on we should be wondering about life after man. A race of sublime, post-human creatures no longer burdened by the injustice of ugliness, and Miami would be their global capital. We would all have the same rounded, innocent brow, skin as soft as satin, almond eyes, everyone would be entitled to long, graceful hands with grey nail varnish, the following would be standard issue: full lips, high cheekbones, velvety ears, impish noses, silky hair, slender perfumed necks and especially pointy elbows. Elbows for everyone! Come on, let's democratize elbows. As Paulina Prizkova humbly recognized in an interview: 'I'm very happy that people think I'm pretty but it's just a question of mathematics: the number of millimetres between my eyes and my chin.'

Charlie and I stand in the sea making our endless phone calls. We drive around the beach in giant Jeeps. Despite Browning's death, we haven't cancelled the Yoplite shoot, too much money having already been spent on the production. At one point, Charlie took a little box out of his pocket. It contained a few grams of Mark Browning's ashes. It's what Mark would have wanted: to float off on the waves in Miami. There were a few traces of ash left in his palm, and I had an idea. I asked him to hold out his arm and open his hand in the sunlight. I leaned over. And that's how I sniffed what was left of my friend, my mentor, Mark Browning! I've got Browning all around my brain!

Let us know if you find a single ugly girl in this town. People who, anywhere else, would be statistically abnormal (beautiful and muscular) are the norm here, to the extent that they almost become boring (don't let's forget that I'm a great advocate of boredom). There's always a girl who's younger and prettier than the last. But envy is one of the seven deadly sins. Miami, twinned with Sodom, Gomorra and Babylon!

There's a man in Coconut Grove taking his six Chihuahuas for a walk on the lead and scooping up their shit with a plastic glove. He passes men trafficking salsa, and youngsters slaloming along on roller-skates. Groups of bronzed creatures talking into their cell-phones outside the Colony. We come to realize that in Miami we're in the middle of a giant advertisement. It's not advertising that imitates life, it's life that imitates advertising. Pink Cadillacs with neon lighting on the floor vibrate to the rhythm of Chicano rap. So much beauty and wealth can't help but make your head spin. In the News Café we gaze from one top model to the next, thinking, 'What a face, what grace, what a figure', but we're really wishing they were defaced, disgraced and disfigured.

The Art Deco district of Miami is on the south side of town, by the sea. It was built in the 1930s for retired people. In the early 1940s a lot of soldiers were mobilized to Miami because the US Army was afraid the Japanese might attack Florida. Then Batista's fall from power in 1959 brought a big influx of Cubans. Miami, therefore, has a mixture of the retired (pension-fund holders for whom every salaried man and woman in the Western world toils all year long), the military (who protect them) and the Cubans (who drug them): the perfect cocktail. In the 1970s the petrol crisis calmed things down in the town. Everybody thought it was finished, outdated, a has-been, right up until an ad relaunched the place fifteen years later, in 1985.

That year Bruce Weber shot a series of photos for Calvin Klein on Ocean Drive. When these few pages of advertising appeared in international magazines they instantly turned Miami into the fashion capital of the world. Miami is the town with a photographer for a prince. If the Nazis had benefited from the advertising clout of somewhere like that, they would have killed ten times more people. Christy Turlington was discovered on the beach there by a talent scout. Then there was Gianni Versace, who made all his catalogues there, before being assassinated there on 15 July 1997. Creatures on roller-skates, copper-coloured Cubans, gays in shorts, glide along the pavements hiding behind their latest-model Oakley shades. These things are not contradictory. The Nazis have won now: even black people dye their hair blond. We all strive to look like the joyful Hitlerjugend, with chocolate-bar abdomens. The anti-Semites have got what they wanted: Woody Allen makes girls laugh but they'd still rather sleep with the blond Aryan Brad Pitt.

Sheltering under a manicured palm tree, we watch the Volleypalooza, a two-day volleyball tournament held on the beach between the modelling agencies. Peter String-fellow and Hugh Heffner referee. (As indeed they referee the planet on the 363 other days in the year.) Perfections in red and black bikinis smash the ball on to the burning-hot sand. Droplets of sweat and sea water flick from their golden hair and land in the creamy navels of their laughing friends. Every now and then the light breeze coming up off the ocean gives them goose-pimples; even from where we're standing, we can revel in the sight of their delicately shivering arms. The sand scattered by their frail shoulders shines like a shower of fine sequins. The whole spectacle makes our hearts ache with monotonous languor. What kills us the most is their white teeth. If only I'd recorded an album which sold a million copies, we wouldn't have come to this. Oh, by the way, it was the red-bikini team who won the Volleypalooza. The captain of the winning team is fifteen; next to her Cameron Diaz, Uma Thurman, Gisele Bundchen and Kate Moss are just four old tuna fish. And stop thinking that all we want to do is screw these resplendent creatures. We couldn't really give a stuff about their vaginas. What we'd actually like to do is to brush their eyelids with our lips, to skim their foreheads with the tips of our fingers, to lie alongside them, to listen to them telling us about their childhood in Arizona or South Carolina; what we want is to watch a soap on TV and sit cracking cashew nuts with them and just, from time to time, to put a wayward lock of hair back behind their ear. Do you see what I mean or not? Oh, we'd know how to take care of you, ordering sushi on room service, dancing slow to 'Protection' by Massive Attack, laughing when we talk about our school days, yes, because we have the same memories as them (the first time we got drunk on beer, the ridiculous haircuts, the first love which is of course also the last, the denim jackets, the parties, the cider, *Star Wars*, all that), but these gorgeous girls always prefer gay bookers and Ferrari drivers and that's why this planet is going so wrong. No, I haven't got a sexual obsession, but there isn't a word for being obsessed by your lungs. Or perhaps there is: I've got a 'pulmonary obsession', there you are.

In the evening we have dinner with some not-quite-top models on a hired yacht. After dessert, Enrique Innizass bets one of them $1,000 that she won't take off her knickers and throw them on to the ceiling to see if they'll stick. The girl proceeds to do so and we all laugh, even though it's not really very funny (her knickers fall back down on to the dish of spaghetti). The whole world is prostituted. To pay or to be paid, that is the question. Grosso mouldo, you're paid until you're about forty; after that, you pay others, that's the way it goes – there is no appeals procedure with the Court of Physical Beauty. Playboys with their four-day stubble look to see if we're looking at them, and we look at them looking to see if we're looking at them, and they look at us looking at them looking to see if we're looking at them, and it's an endless ballet a bit like the Hall of Mirrors, an old fairground attraction, a sort of labyrinth of mirrors where you keep bumping into your own reflection. I remember that, as children, we would come out covered in bumps and bruises from head-butting ourselves so often.

25

Ocean Drive, with its neon electrocuting the fluorescent passers-by. The warm wind carries flyers about soirées that have been and gone. The night before in the Living Room, the girls danced like slabs of meat. (If you get into the Living Room, then you must be a VIP. Once inside, if you have a table, then you must be a VVIP. If there's a bottle of champagne on your table, then you must be a VVVIP. And if the owner comes and kisses you on the mouth, then either you're a VVVVIP or you're Madonna.) Miami Beach is an enormous sweetie shop: the buildings look like ice creams and the girls are like sweets you'd like to feel melting slowly on your tongue.

Wake up at six a.m. to do the filming in the best light of the day. We've rented a billionaire's house at Key Biscayne, with copies of Tamara de Lempicka paintings on the walls. Tamara (our one) has taken to her new life as an ad star very quickly. She has her hair and make-up done and she's plied with coffee in the production trailer. The set decorators are put to work tinting the lawn (which isn't green enough in relation to the story-board). The director of photography gives instructions no one understands to a very understanding team of technicians. They spend their time measuring the light levels, exchanging arcane figures.

'Try to get to 12 on the 4.'

'No, we'll try with a different focal length. Can you give me the 8 in 14?'

Charlie and I just eat everything that catering offers us: chewing gum, cheese-flavoured ice creams, bubble gum, salmon burgers, chewing gum of salmon and cheese ice cream with chicken and sashimis. Suddenly it's half past eight and Enrique's stopped smiling.

'The sky is-e white, we can't-e film in this-a weather.'

The client made it very clear that he wanted blue skies and shadows.

'What-e can I do,' he went on, 'if God-e gives me this-e sort of light-a?'

To which Charlie retorts imperiously, 'God is an appalling director of photography.'

You can't do anything about a white sky in the editing suite. If we filmed in these conditions, it would have to be coloured frame by frame, at $6,000 a day. So we have breakfast ten times while we wait for the mist to disperse. The TV producer is tearing her hair out while she calls the insurance company the other side of the Atlantic to open a 'Weather Day' umbrella. For my part, I'm not panicking. Since I stopped the coke, I eat the whole time.

Tamara and Charlie and I are like the *Jules et Jim* of Florida. The Yanks keep asking us, 'Are you playing a *ménage à trois?*'

We drink Corona all morning and can't stop laughing. Everyone falls in love with Tamara. She's getting £6,000 a day to provoke this sort of chemical reaction in every male. There are bearded men wearing safety helmets and carrying cables, walkie-talkies crackling to themselves, lighting engineers peering up at the sky impotently, and wc smother ourselves in total sun-block to attract the sun. There are black screens protecting us from reality; the world is blocked off. But without the sun, what the hell's the point of Miami?

'We'll have to avoid having palm trees in the shot. This is meant to be Europe, don't let's forget. Or we'll have to arrange to have a matt-painting done of beeches and oaks.'

'Congratulations for that comment, Octave, you've just made yourself useful. In one sentence you've justified the price of your air ticket.'

Charlie's joking but he seems preoccupied. He's been on the brink of saying something all morning. Is he finally going to spit it out? Yup.

'You know, Octave, I've got something to tell you. There are going to be some big changes at the agency.'

'Yes, thank you. Considering the art director has died, that's highly probable.'

'You don't say the art director has died, you say the art director is deceased.'

'Are you proposing to make a joke about our beloved colleague's suicide?'

Tamara's laughing but Charlie carries on in the same vein.

'Did you notice that Jeff didn't go to Senegal?'

'Yes, and when I realized he wasn't going, I felt like

cancelling my trip. I don't know how we managed to survive four days without him.'

'Stop mucking about. I know where he was, where Jeff was while we were farting about on the hotel dance floor. The dear boy was in New York, would you believe, asking the powers that be at The Ross for Philip's job, the chairman's job for God's sake.'

'What the hell are you saying?'

'Oh, he played his cards very cleverly, did little Jeff. He went to head office with backing from Dewler at Damione, and he told them that we'd lose that budget if we didn't change our team of directors in London. And do you know what the big shots said?'

'Go fuck yourself, Jeff?'

'Indeed not. The Yanks love that sort of thing, the pushy, hungry young achiever shouldering out the old – they teach that to their sharks at Harvard and in every Western with John Wayne.'

'Now, hang on a minute, you've got to be joking. Did you make all this up yourself?'

Charlie chews on a fingernail and doesn't look like someone revelling in the yarn they've just spun.

'Octavio, you were so busy taking notes for your book that you forgot to watch what was going on around you.'

'Hey, hey, that's just great coming from you, seeing you sit surfing the Net all day, digging up your sick photos.'

'Not at all, I'm learning about the age in which I live. While we're on the subject, remind me to show you the film of the ninety-year-old woman eating her own shit. Well, anyway. Did you see the way they all flipped at the seminar? Wake up. Jeff is going to be made chairman of The Ross instead of Philip, who'll take responsibility for Europe, which is a non-post. They'll call him "Chairman Emeritus", or something like that, to let him down gently.'

'*Jeff, boss of the agency?* But he's not even thirty. He's just a child!'

'Perhaps, but he's not sweet and innocent in my opinion. Welcome to the new millennium, partner. It's fashionable to have chairmen of thirty. They're just as bad as the fifty-year-olds but they look better and cost less. That's why the Yankee shareholders rubber-stamped him. He had the support of the biggest budget the agency's got. Jeff couldn't fail. Anyway, Jeff couldn't stand Browning. Do you see what I mean?'

'Fuck! You mean Mark's gone and killed himself because he knew that little shit was going to chuck him out on to the streets?'

'Of course. And he was pretty sure that we were going to nab his job.'

The sky can be as white as it likes but don't let it fall in like this.

'I must have heard that wrong. You mean Jeff's appointing us as creative directors?'

'Jeff rang me this morning to offer us the job. It's a massive amount a month each plus expenses, the flat and the Porsche.'

Tamara smiles.

'Octave, sweetheart, for someone who wanted to get himself fired, things aren't turning out that well, are they?'

'Hey, you and your creature comforts, shut it, OK?'

'You're right, darling. You're crea-tive and I'm just a crea-ture.'

'That's cute,' Charlie says curtly, 'but you've got it all wrong, my sweet. We're not just on the creative team now, we're the directors. There's a difference.'

'Hey, hang on. I didn't say I'd accepted the offer.'

'It is una offer that-e ee-you cannot-e refuse,' cuts in Enrique, because the whole production team obviously knew about this, except for me.'

And that's just when the sun decides to come out, cheeky bugger.

26

You would really have thought that Tamara had been acting all her life – if you think about it, she had actually. Being a call girl prepares you for being an actress far more efficiently than the Actors' Studio. She turns out to be perfectly at ease in front of the camera. She seduces the lens while she spoons her pot of yoghurt greedily as if her life depended on it. She's never been more dazzling than in this false Mediterranean garden transposed to Florida.

'She's *the* girl of the new century,' the local technical director announces sententiously to the chick filming the 'making of'. I think he wants a) to introduce her to John Casablanca at Elite and b) to take her from behind. But not necessarily in that order.

We're invading a foreign country before besieging their media. The Yoplite campaign will stay on the air until 2004 and will appear in several forms: the 4m x 3m hoarding posters, the bus-shelter posters, ads in women's magazines, in-store advertising, promotional offers, painted walls, competitions, factual leaflets, advertorials, Internet sites, tie-in displays and money-back offers on presentation of proof of purchase. Tamara, you will be everywhere, you will become the emblem for the leading fat-free fromage frais in the global market.

We drink Cape Cods while we talk to the make-up girl about Aspen. We meet a few skinny cows (the nickname we've given to the anorexic grungettes trying to get heroin on Washington Avenue). We act out dramatic deaths in front of Gianni Versace's house. Some tourists take our picture as we grovel on the ground under the machine-gun fire. We swathe ourselves in the white tenting at the Delano Hotel: Tamara becomes Scheherazade and I become Caspar, the friendly ghost. The people around us are so narcissistic that they no longer make love with anyone but themselves. How would you define a good day in Miami? One-third roller-skating, one-third ecstasy and one-third masturbation.

On the set the lawn has been burned dry by the sun again. To get it back to green the props girls are spraying it with food dye. There's a drag-queen wrestling competition at the Score on Lincoln Road this evening: cross-dressers pull each other's wigs off in the ring. 'Nothing really matters,' sings Madonna, who has a house here. She's summed the problem up pretty well. I love Tamara and I love Sophie; with an art director's salary, I could easily afford to keep them both. But I really can't accept an offer which goes against everything I said on the first page of this book, the one where I said, 'I'm writing this book to get myself fired.' Or I'd have to alter that and put, 'I'm writing this book to get myself promoted' . . . Tamara interrupts my thoughts.

'Would you like coffee, tea or me?'

'All three in my mouth. Tell me, what's your favourite ad, Tamara?'

'LESS FLOWER, MORE POWER. It's the slogan for the new Volkswagen Beetle.'

'You don't say "slogan", you say "hook". Remember that if you want me to give you a job.'

We spend the afternoon lolling in front of the combo, a Sony monitor which transmits every take: Tamara on the terrace, Tamara on the steps, Tamara in the garden, Tamara in long shot, Tamara in close-up, Tamara naturally artificial, Tamara looking at the camera, Tamara artificially natural, Tamara tasting the product (the opening of the pot, the plunging in of the spoon, the oral delectation), Tamara and her emotive elbow, Tamara and her the-best breasts. But the Tamara I like best is reserved for me, and that's Tamara wearing nothing but flip-flops, on my bedroom balcony, with a ring on one of the toes of her left foot and a rose tattooed above her right breast. The one I can say things like this to: 'I don't want to make love to you but you just make me happy. I think I love you, Tamara. You've got big feet but I love you. You're better when you're computer enhanced than in the flesh but I love you.'

'I know a lot of creeps who pretend to be nice, but you're a rare specimen: a nice guy who pretends to be a creep. Kiss me. It won't cost you anything this time.'

'Can love be measured by the hours in a day? I have no answers now but this much I can say: I know I'll need you till the stars all burn away . . .'

'More words, it's always words.'

*

The tasting shot is always the most difficult part of the job: in the blazing sun, after lunch, the poor girl had to simulate ecstasy twenty times as she put a spoonful of Yoplite into her mouth. After a few takes she was absolutely sick of the stuff. So the props girl brought her a little basin she could spit it into as soon as Enrique called, 'Cut!' There, a little revelation we can entrust to you, don't tell too many people: every time you see an actor savouring some food product in an ad, you should know that they never swallow it but spew it straight out into a specially provided receptacle as soon as the camera stops rolling.

Charlie and I are sitting on plastic chairs with only great piles of junk food for company. It's the same circus on every commercial shoot. The creative team are parked in a corner and mollycoddled with utter contempt, in the hopes that they won't find the need to say too much on the pretext that they're the *auteurs* of the campaign which is being committed to celluloid. We feel humiliated, useless and bloated on sweets and cakes – just a bit more sick at heart than usual, then. We pretend not to notice anything because we know that, as future art directors of The Ross London, we'll have a thousand opportunities to take our implacable revenge.

We'll be rich, unjust and cruel.

We'll fire our old friends.

We'll blow hot and cold to terrorize all our employees.

We'll take credit for the ideas of our subordinates.

We'll hire young directors to get all their fresh ideas by dangling the carrot of some big job which we'll actually do ourselves behind their backs.

We'll refuse to grant any holiday time to salaried staff before we've spent our own holidays in Mauritius.

We'll be megalomaniacs and we'll be as obscene as we please.

We'll keep the best clients for ourselves and we'll give the most irresistible campaigns to freelancers outside the company so that the in-house team are well and truly depressed.

We'll insist on having our photos on the business pages of *The Times*, then we'll demand that the journalist concerned is fired as soon as they appear if the paper doesn't canonize us sufficiently (by threatening that we won't buy any more ad space).

We'll personify a complete revolution in advertising.

We'll pay a press officer so that we can be quoted in the pages of *Campaign* saying, 'It's important to distinguish between the concept and the precept.'

We'll also us the word 'pre-empt' very frequently.

We'll be snowed under with work and completely uncontactable; people will have to wait at least three months for a meeting with us (and then they'll be cancelled at the last minute, the morning before the meeting, by an arrogant secretary).

We'll button our shirts right up to the top.

We'll spawn epidemics of nervous breakdowns all around us. People will say terrible things about us in the profession but never to our faces because everyone will be afraid of us.

We won't do a stroke of work, but our nearest and dearest will stop seeing us all the same.

We'll be dangerous and completely superfluous.
We'll be pulling the strings of modern society.
We'll stay in the shade 'even in broad daylight'.
We'll be proud to have such important irresponsibilities.

'Is everything OK with the make-up?'

Our extravagant cat-who-got-the-cream daydream is interrupted by the make-up girl, who needs a detailed opinion. When the time comes we'll make her chief make-up artist for the whole R & C group because she managed to recognize how important we are even before we've been appointed.

'We just need something very natural,' says Charlie peremptorily. 'She needs to look healthy/balanced/dynamic/authentic.'

'Yeah, I'll do her lips kinda glossy. I won't even touch her colouring. She has such beautiful skin.'

'Not glossy,' Charlie insists with all the assurance of the future boss that he is, 'I prefer shiny.'

'Of course, shiny is better than glossy,' I'm quick to agree. 'Otherwise we'll be tending towards an excess in terms of colour.'

The make-up girl backs off respectfully from two such specialists of labial cosmetics – visible pros whom nobody should mess with. All we need to do now is to snub the culinary stylist and *tutto* will be absolutely *bene*.

The whole crew is turned on by Tamara. We all adore her and exchange conspiratorial winks about her celestial beauty. We could have been happy if I hadn't spent my time thinking about someone else. Why is it that I only want people who aren't there? Every now and then Tamara lays her hands on my face; I find it soothing. I really needed to lighten up. Hey, now that would be a good emergency baseline: 'YOPLITE. BECAUSE WE ALL NEED TO LIGHTEN UP SOMETIMES'. I jot it down, you never know.

'So, are you going to accept all this money you're being offered?'

'Money doesn't make you happy, Tamara, you know that.'

'Thanks to you, yes, I do know that now. I didn't know before. To know that money doesn't make you happy, you have to know them both: money and happiness, I mean.'

'Do you want to marry me?'

'No, well, yes, but on one condition: at the wedding we'll have a helicopter which drops a shower of pink marsh-mallows.'

'And what do we do with the white ones?'

'We eat them!'

Why's she looking away? We're both a bit embarrassed. I take her hand, which is covered in little hennaed patterns.

'What? What is it?'

'It's not nice of you to be so nice. I preferred it when you pretended to be a creep.'

'But . . .'

'Stop it. You know you don't love me. I'd like to be friv-olous like you, it's just I'm fed up with playing games, you know. I've thought about things and I think I'm going to give it all up. With the money from Yoplite, I could buy myself a little house in Morocco. I've got my daughter to bring up. I've left her over there with my mother and I miss her so much . . . Listen, Octave, you've got to get back together with your girlfriend and look after your child. She's giving you the most beautiful thing anyone can give another person. You should accept it.'

'Shit. What is it with all of you? As soon as things are going well, you feel you have to start talking about babies! Instead of addressing the question 'Why should we go on with life?' you seem to prefer perpetuating the problem!'

'Pack it in with your two-bit philosophy. You shouldn't make jokes like that with me. My daughter hasn't even got a father.'

'So what? My father didn't bring me up either and I'm not making a great drama out of it.'

'Hang on, have you had a good look at yourself? You dump a girl who's carrying your baby so that you can spend your time with hookers!'

'Yeah, well . . . at least I'm free.'

'Free? Come on, I must be dreaming! Don't give me that, Octave, not from you! Holy fuck! You're just so second millennium! Look me in the eye, I said in the eye. This child that's going to be born *could* have a father. For the first time in your life, you can actually do something. How long are you going to last like this, hanging around in tacky nightclubs, listening to the same dirty jokes told by the same stupid, impotent piss artists? How long, for fuck's sake? Is that your idea of freedom?'

There are psychoanalysts who'll cost you $150 a session; Tamara is a moralist at £300 an hour.

'Give me a break with your morals! Christ!'

'Stop attacking me, you're doing my head in. Morals

may not be very fashionable, but they're still the best we've been able to come up with for separating good from evil.'

'So what? I'd rather be a complete bastard but free – yes, free, that's what I said – than ethical but trapped! I understand perfectly well what you're saying but, believe it or not, a happy family life can be even more pathetic than some filthy, smutty story told by a drunken idiot at six o'clock in the morning. Do you see what I'm saying? And anyway, how do you expect me to bring up a child when I can't help falling in love with some hooker every two minutes, for fuck's sake! Oops.'

By saying that I've infringed one of the ground rules with Tamara. She's the only one who's allowed to use the word 'hooker'; if someone else does, she takes it as an insult. She dissolves into tears. I try to backtrack.

'Don't cry. I'm sorry, you're a saint, you know that. I've told you so many times. I'm already the first man who pays girls not to sleep with them, now I'm also the first to make a working girl cry. Now that's something to be proud of, isn't it? Can I borrow your mobile, I've got to let the *Guinness Book of Records* know. Yes, hello? Could you put me through to the Most Untactful Man in the World department please?'

Bingo: she's beginning to smile; the make-up girl will only have a bit of mascara to touch up. I carry on with my self-analysis now that I've got started.

'My beloved immigrant, can you explain something for me. Why is it that, as soon as you love a woman and everything's going fantastically, she wants to turn you into a child-minder, to put strings of children between you, an army of rugrats screaming under your feet and stopping you spending time alone together? For God's sake, is it so terrifying being just the two of you? I really liked being a DINKy couple (Dual Income No Kids), why would anyone want to turn that into a FAMILy (Fabrication of Artificial Misery of Inderterminate Length)? Don't you think having children is absolutely pitiful? All those romantic couples who no longer talk about anything but dirty nappies? Do you think the Gallagher brothers are sexy now that they're wiping their children's arses? You'd have to have a poo-fixation! And anyway, there isn't room for a baby's car seat in my BMW Z3 coupé!'

'You're the one that's pitiful. If your mother hadn't had any children, you wouldn't be here to rant on like that with all this crap.'

'That wouldn't be much of a loss!!'

'Shut up!!'

'Shut up to you too!!'

'OH, AND FOR CHRIST'S SAKE, GIVE ME A BREAK WITH YOUR EXCLAMATION MARKS!!!!!' she exclaimed with a sniff.

She blew her nose. Oh, God, but she's beautiful when she cries. If men hurt women so much, it's probably because they're so much more beautiful when they cry.

She looks up and then finds the words that will convince me.

'We could still see each other on the quiet.'

Long live that brand of morality. It was Blaise Pascal who said, 'True morality puts no store by morality.' And, as I sucked up her tears with the straw from my Seven Up, we both thought the same thing.

'Do you know why things'll never work out between us two?'

'Yes, I do,' I said. 'Because I'm not free and you're too free.'

27

And then the filming's over. We've just spent $750,000 in three days. Before we packed away the cameras we asked Enrique to make a trash version of the ad. OK, so we were pissed, so was Tamara, and Charlie started yelling.

'Listen. LISTEN TO ME, ALL OF YOU! Just listen, please. Last time I saw Mark Browning alive, he was giving Octave here a hard time, telling him the script that we've just been shooting was crap and that he had to write another one.'

'It's true,' I added. 'He even said these words, which will remain engraved on my mind till my dying day: "You can never hide from the possibility of finding a better campaign."'

'Ladies and gentlemen, are we going to ignore the last wishes of a dead man?'

The technicians weren't 100 per cent supportive. After a few negotiations with the TV producer and Enrique, a decision was nevertheless made to shoot a quick 'agency' take, shot in sequence with a camera on the shoulder, Dogma-style (that winter just everything had to be filmed to match the intellectual Danish label).

Here's what the 'Yoplite Dogma' version was like. Tamara is wandering around a teak-panelled interior. She gracefully takes off her T-shirt on the veranda and then, stripped to the waist, she looks at the camera as she smears the yoghurt on to her cheeks and her breasts. She twirls on the spot and then gambols barefoot through the garden as she starts to yell at her fat-free yoghurt, 'Yoplite, I'm gonna eat you!' Then she rolls in the newly repainted grass, her breasts are covered in green paint and Yoplite, and she licks the fromage frais from her top lip with a moan of pleasure (zoom in on her face, dripping with the product). 'Mmmm. . . . Yoplite. It's so good when it comes in your mouth.'

What talent. We decide to send this version to the International Festival of Advertising in Cannes without showing it to Damione. If we get a Lion for it, Dewler will have to join in the applause.

Browning would have appreciated such devotion. We can go home with a clear conscience and settle into his chair, which has barely had time to cool. But that's not enough for Charlie, who's obviously determined to be more impregnable than ever. That same evening, after the end-of-shoot party at the Liquid, he leads us off on the merry dance that I am, unfortunately, constrained to relate to you here.

28

The strobes carved the room into blocks of movement. An old sado-masochist crossed the dance floor wearing a corset which gave her a six-inch waist measurement. She looked like an hourglass in black leather.

'D'you know what that old bat makes me think? In Europe, there are companies making thousands of people unemployed just so that they can cough up more money for retired Americans in Miami, aren't there?'

'Uh . . . pretty much, yes. The old people in Florida are all shareholders in the pension funds which own international companies, so basically, yes.'

'Well, then, seeing as we're here, why don't we go and see one of these old buggers who own the planet? I mean, it would be stupid to be in their town and not give one of them a piece of our mind. Perhaps we could even persuade them not to fire anyone next time, hey. What d'you think?'

'I think you're pissed, but OK, let's do it.'

And so off we went, Tamara, Charlie and myself, through the streets of Miami Vice, on the lookout for a representative of the global shareholders.

*

Ding! Dong! Ding! Dong-Ding-Dong-Ding-Dong-Ding!

In Miami even the doorbells try to get noticed: this one plays *Eine kleine Nachtmusik* instead of just ringing like everyone else's. We've been wandering aimlessly round the Coral Gables residential neighbourhood for an hour looking for a pension-fund holder to lecture. Charlie eventually rang at the door of a resplendent Moorish villa.

'Yes?'

'Good evening, madam, could we have a word with you?'

'Well, what's it about? It's very late, you know.'

'Well, you see it's Tamara here.' Tamara smiles at the surveillance camera. 'She says that she's your granddaughter, Mrs Ward.'

Bzzz.

The door opens to reveal a mummie. Well, a thing which must have been a woman a very long time ago, in a very distant galaxy. Nose, mouth, eyes, forehead, cheeks completely filled out with collagen. The rest of the body looks like a wrinkled potato – an analogy which probably owes a lot to the nature of the dressing gown wrapped round it.

'It's only her skin that's been pulled,' announced Charlie rather heavily.

'What were you saying? What granddaughter? I . . .'

Too late. The old woman didn't have time to complain before Tamara knocked her to the floor (she's a judo brown-belt). We go into the colossal gilded house. Everything that isn't gold is white marble. Wow. Tamara and Charlie carry Mrs Ward to a sofa covered in psychedelic patterns – it must have been fashionable at about the same time as its owner, probably at some time in the twentieth century.

'So, now that we understand each other so well, Mrs Wardthingy, you're going to listen to us like a good girl. Do you live here alone?'

'Yes, I mean, no, not at all. The police will be here any minute. HELP! HEEEELP!'

'Let's gag her. Tamara, give me your scarf?'

'Here.'

She stuffs her bandanna into her mouth, and Charlie sits on her, and I can assure you that he's as leaden as his jokes. At last the old dear's going to be able to listen to what he has to say in silence.

'You see, my dear, we happen to have come to you but we could have gone to any number of other people responsible for contemporary misery. You have to realize that from now on this sort of visit is going to become quite commonplace. It's high time the shareholders of American pension funds realized that they just can't keep ruining the lives of millions of innocent people with impunity, without paying their share of suffering sooner or later, do I make myself clear?'

Charlie's on a roll. It's always like that with the quiet ones. Once they open up, you can't stop them.

'Have you heard of a book called *Journey to the End of Night* by Celine?'

'Mpffghpffhmmghphh.'

'No, not the Celine who sang the *Titanic* theme tune. I might be being a tad obscure here for you, Mrs Ward, but Celine was a French writer. The hero of his most famous novel was called Bardamu and he went all round the world looking for someone to blame. He lives through war, poverty and illness, he goes to Africa and to America, but he never finds anyone responsible for our desolate state. The book was published in 1932 and five years later Celine found himself a scapegoat: the Jews.'

Tamara's having a good look round the house, peeps in the fridge, gets herself a beer and brings us one each. I'm making notes on Charlie's speech as he carries on holding forth, sitting astride the mummie on her hideous sofa.

'Now, we all know that Celine rather lost his way by descending to the level of ignoble anti-Semitism – and forgive me the pleonasm. And yet we too, like Bardamu, are all looking for someone to take responsibility. This young woman here is called Tamara, and she would like to know why she has to sell her arse so that she can send money out to her little girl. This cretin with me is called Octave, and he too keeps asking himself questions, as indeed you can see from the consumptive gargoyle that serves as his face. What is causing this rot in the world? Who *are* the baddies? Is it the Serbs? Or the Russian Mafia? The Islamic Fundamentalists? The Colombian cartels? Scapegoats, all of them! Like the "Judaeo-Masonic conspiracy" of the 1930s! Do you see what I'm driving at, Lady Thingamajig? You are our scapegoat. It's important for each and every one of us on this earth to understand the consequences of our actions. If, for example, I buy products from Monsanto, I'm endorsing genetically modified organisms and the privatization of agricultural seed production. You entrusted your savings to a financial group which pays you enough interest for you to live in this monstrous villa in a beautiful part of Miami. It's highly likely that you didn't put much thought into the consequences of this decision, which for you was anodyne but for us sealed our fates, do you understand? Because this decision made you *Queen of the world.*'

Charlie taps her cheek so that she opens her eyes, which are brimming with tears. The old girl is making plaintive little cries, muffled by the scarf.

'You know,' he went on, 'when I was little I used to love James Bond films, and there was always a baddy who wanted to rule the world, so he would train up his secret army, hidden in an underground fortress, and he always threatened to blow up the planet with nuclear missiles stolen from Uzbekistan. Do you remember those films, Mrs What's-yer-name? Well, I discovered recently that James Bond, just like my French friend Celine, was just kidding himself. The King of the World isn't like that at all really. Funny, isn't it? The King of the World has a cheap old bathrobe, a crap house, a blue wig, a mouth full of bandanna, and on top of that he doesn't even know he's King of the World! It's you, Mrs Wardikins! And do you know who we are? We're 007! Da na da na da der da, da-na da-na da der daaa!'

Charlie renders John Barry's theme tune (or is it Monty Norman's – £30,000 in damages says it is). He's perfectly in tune but that doesn't stop the Queen of the World from blubbing pathetically with her head buried in her garish-coloured Versace-style cushion (the man can't be dead, his work lives on).

'Don't try to make me feel sorry for you, Mrs Ward-my-arse. Did you feel sorry when entire regions were devastated by large-scale cutbacks, intensive restructuring and abusive social programmes intended for your eyes only? So no mucking about, if you please. A bit of dignity and everything will be fine. My name is Bond, James Bond. We only came here to ask you to tell your Templeton pension fund, which manages $200 billion, that from now on it won't be able to claim the same return from its companies, because otherwise more and more people like us will come to call on people like you, OK?'

That's when Tamara intervened.

'Charlie, wait, I think she's trying to show you something.'

The old girl was indeed pointing her pudgy fingers at a framed photograph on the coffee table. It was a black-and-white picture of a handsome soldier in the US Army, smiling in his smart peaked cap.

'Mmfhghmfphhgg!!!' she bellowed, pointing at the picture.

I pulled the bandanna from her mouth so that we could hear what Mmfhghmfphhgg meant a bit more clearly. She started screaming at the top of her lungs.

'WE SAVED YOUR ASS IN '44! MY HUSBAND DIED IN NOR-FUCKING-MANDY!! Look, you ASS-HOLE, look at MY HUSBAND, who died in FUCKING EUROPE on D-DAY!!'

Personally, I thought she had a point. But it was then that Charlie completely lost it. I didn't know about his family background. First I'd heard of it, honest.

'Listen, Miss. We're not going to start chucking our war dead in each other's faces all evening. You only got into that war so that you could export Coca-Cola. *It's Coca-Cola that killed your husband!* But my father committed suicide because he was fired from his company so that they could make bigger profits. I found him hanging, do you understand that, you bitch? YOU KILLED MY FATHER!'

He was slapping her a bit too hard. The old woman's nose was bleeding. I swear I tried to hold him back, but the alcohol made him ten times stronger than normal.

'YOU TOPPED MY FATHER, YOU OLD COW, YOU CAN PAY FOR IT NOW!'

He was thrashing her now, aiming for her eyes with his fists, breaking his beer bottle over her nose, punching out her dentures and sticking them up her cunt. Well, fine, you could also say that he'd decided to cut short a life of suffering and one which had, anyway, pretty much come to term, but it strikes me that you could also call it losing it. Anyway, after about five minutes (which is a very long time – a boxing round, for example, doesn't last that long), Mrs Ward was no longer breathing and a smell of shit permeated the room. The Versace cover was ripe for dry-cleaning.

Apparently accustomed to such losses of 'it', Tamara didn't bat an eyelid. Having taken Mrs Ward's pulse, in other words confirmed that she was deceased, she started methodically tidying up the mess as quickly as possible. She gave us instructions to put the old woman's body at the foot of her Graeco-Roman staircase. Then we left the sordid villa on tiptoe, not before we'd destroyed the surveillance camera with stones from the garden.

'D'you think it's recording?'

'No, it's just an intercom.'

'Anyway, even if they tried to trace us, no one knows us here.'

That sentence caused considerable mirth among the duty watchmen who reviewed the various security monitors. They were rather less amused when they realized that Mrs Ward had succumbed in the assault and that they would have to file a report to the Miami Police Department.

That was when I stopped thinking. The neighbourhood was deserted. Charlie had come back to his senses. He'd had to agree with Tamara.

'Her sofa really was crap, though, wasn't it.'

We ended the evening at the Club Madonna, a strip club where the dancers (sort of cyberwomen perfectly rebuilt from pared-down component parts) used their mouths to tug $10 bills from between your flies. We cheered their unbelievable breasts – hardly surprising they were un-believable, they weren't real.

'That's always the way with women,' said Charlie, 'either they frustrate you or they disgust you.'

This piqued Tamara's professional pride and she then treated us to the most magnificent show, standing up on the bar, sucking the neck of her Corona and hardening her nipples with the ice cubes from my vodka, until we were chucked out for giving the resident floor show too much competition. Then the three of us fell asleep in front of the hotel's 'pay per view' TV, which had an excellent porn show featuring, notably, an anal double-fisting, something I didn't know was technically possible, and I have to confess that the actress's cries made me come in my trousers.

The following morning, as we got on to the flight back to London (still in Business Class at £3,500 a seat, with 'nest of buckwheat pasta garnished with caviar and drizzled with jus of cherry tomatoes' on the menu), Charlie told me that he was going to accept the post of CD. I prayed for the plane to crash but, as usual, it did nothing of the kind. And that's how I ended up in the space of a day being the head of an advertising agency and an accessory to murder.

29

Back in London we found the following e-mail on our computers. It had been sent to every employee of Rosserys & Crow world-wide:

Dear friends in the Rosserys & Crow group,

One of my principal obligations to our clients, our shareholders and each and every one of you is to clarify the future of Rosserys & Crow. In the last few years, we have all been fortunate enough to benefit from an exceptionally strong management team. These talented individuals have made it possible for us to achieve our goals as specialists in global and integrated marketing, and have simultaneously transformed our group of companies into leaders in the forefront of communications. I now recognize their importance in our success, and I am paving the way for Rosserys & Crow's continued vitality in the new millennium.

It is with great pride and satisfaction that I announce the appointment of Jeffrey Parcourt as Chairman of Rosserys London. Philip Englefin has been promoted to Executive Officer for Europe and will have the title Chairman Emeritus. In his role as Chairman Emeritus, Philip will be free to spend more time doing what he loves best – working actively to bring to the marketplace a better quality of communication integrated into our global achievements.

Jeffrey's new appointment will mean that he can concentrate on what he does best – working with us to raise the quality and the strategic innovation which we deem very important to raising our international profile. Jeffrey has successfully breathed new life into the Damione account over the last six years, thanks to his dynamic approach and solid application to his work.

I would like to make a point of thanking Philip personally for his tremendous achievements at the head of our London subsidiary. There is no question that all our European subsidiaries will benefit from his in-depth knowledge of both the marketplace and our portfolio of clients.

Jeffrey was confident that the standard of artistic direction would be best served by appointing Octave Parengo and Charlie Nargood to replace Mark Browning, whose tragic death has shocked friends and colleagues alike. He will inform you of further changes to the organization chart. I would like to take this opportunity to tell Mark's colleagues how much his exceptional grasp of conceptual intuition and creative opportunities has enriched not only the history of this agency but also the evolution of global communications.

I will of course help and support Jeffrey, Octave and Charlie to the full extent of my means, and I know that you will do the same.

When I look at the future of Rosserys & Crow, I do

so with pride and tremendous confidence. The leadership of R & C in the twenty-first century will quite simply remain at the very highest level within the business.

With my sincerest regards
Edward S. Farringer Jr

That dickhead Charlie had said yes for both of us a week before the filming. I just had to sign a few pieces of paper. I told myself that by accepting I might be gaining enough power to change things. I was wrong: power is never given to people who might use it. Anyway, what power? Power's just a fabrication that's had its day. Nowadays power is so diverse and so dilute that the whole system has become impotent. And there we were constantly repeating our Gramscist credo: 'To divert an aeroplane, first you have to get inside it.' What an ironic twist of fate! As we now step into the cockpit, with our grenades in our hands, and as we prepare to give orders to the pilot by threatening him with our machine guns, we discover that there never was a pilot. We wanted to divert a plane that no one knew how to fly.

somebody has to pay . . . see you after this message

The scene takes place at Hampton Court. A big fashion show is about to take place. The crowd is thronging around the entrance, guarded by handsome boys from a local private school in their smart uniforms and red ties. We go into the main hall, which is full to bursting with every VIP in the world.

The lights go out. The guests go 'Aaah'. On the podium, completely naked girls parade to a soundtrack of techno-dirty-metal-hard-acid-house.

The guests go into ecstasies about the sublime naked models: Majestic breasts, pert buttocks, legs that go on for ever, pubic hair reduced to rectangular topiaries. Suddenly they stop in the middle of the catwalk and slip their manicured hands under their armpits, where they find a zip! They then unzip their satiny skin and shed their epidermis, as if peeling off wet-suits. In the crowd, an old duchess faints. A bearded man in sunglasses ejaculates on to the jacket of the man in front of him. A twelve-year-old girl sucks a phallus-shaped ice cream while she strokes her inner thigh.

Under their artificial skins, the top models are made of metal. Cyborgs of tempered steel, shiny metallic androids. One of the girls is completely papered over with £50 notes. Another starts spewing a stream of coins. A third throws out fistfuls of credit cards as if they were confetti. They are robotic money-boxes (one of the girls even produces banknotes from her snatch like a cash dispenser).

Standing ovation from the crowd. The guests moan with pleasure. The atmosphere is electric. The music speeds up to an unbearable pitch. Heads start exploding along the rows of seats. There are a dozen heart attacks and several multiple rapes in the second row.

Packshot with coins raining down on the naked body of an adolescent Thai girl.

Slogan superimposed on the screen: 'WHO COULD ASK FOR MORE: COME IN A WHORE.'

This is followed by the legal notice: 'THAT WAS A PUBLIC INFORMATION FILM FOR THE BORB (The British Organization for the Re-opening of Brothels).

5 You

'In a closed society where everybody's guilty, the only crime is getting caught. In a world of thieves, the only final sin is stupidity'

Hunter S. Thompson,
Fear and Loathing in Las Vegas

30

You're actually rather pleased about your promotion. The terrorized expressions on the faces of the 300 newly employed. The nymphomaniac lips of the ex-indifferent secretaries. The change of tone of your superiors, who are now your inferiors. The instant but genuine camaraderie of those who suddenly find that they're your old brothers-at-arms and have been your friends since for ever. Their deference highlights your difference. But you and Charlie are modest about your triumph. You call a meeting for the entire agency and tell them the following:

'Dear friends, the idea of appointing us as art directors was so incongruous that we couldn't help but accept Jeffrey's offer. It was more courageous to say yes than no. We are prepared to tough out what are going to be difficult times ahead: it won't be easy following in the footsteps of a true genius like Mark . . .' (At this point you pause for over four seconds of deeply moved silence.) 'Also because, although we are in advertising, we're terrified of the public, and we will have to overcome this handicap with your help. Advertising pollutes the world, and it will be our duty to invent an ecological form of communication. We will be – and you, therefore, will be – constrained to be intelligent

.t of respect for the consumer. It's all over for the point-
.ess images on crappy-quality film! We have decided to
open up the agency to new creative talents: unknown
authors, forsaken poets, rejected sitcom-writers, directors
of porn films. The time has come for advertising to re-
establish links with the artistic avant-garde of its time. The
Ross must go back to being the experimental laboratory
that it was at its inception. We will strive to measure up to
the degree of creative ambition that has always typified this
organization.

'We will, therefore, begin by introducing a few symbolic
measures with immediate effect. First and foremost, we will
have loudspeakers playing Tina Turner's "Simply the Best"
throughout the day, and this will also be played to anyone
who is put on hold on our telephone system. The telephone
operators and receptionists in the entrance lobby will be
stripped to the waist. All campaign presentations will be
made on our clients' premises by comic actors recruited
from stand-up shows, accompanied by a small Russian
ensemble to create atmosphere. All employees of The Ross
must – and this is imperative – kiss each other on the mouth
in greeting. Every member of the creative team will be
given a Sony PC1 camera so that they can create all the
images that pop into their heads.

'We must rediscover our original innocence, the infancy
of art. We must be constantly *amazed, bedazzled*. We need
to break down this self-serving system, otherwise we won't
get through to people any more. We'd be throwing our
brand names' money out of the window. Never forget, and
this will be our conclusion, that you are here for *your own*

amusement, and that it's by amusing *yourselves* that you're most likely to amuse our buyers. The Ross London's new motto comes from Terence Conran: 'People don't know what they want until you give it to them.' We will have it engraved above the main entrance first thing tomorrow morning. Thank you for your attention and may the party go on!'

The applause was substantial if not spontaneous. You invited your 300 new subordinates for a drink on the terrace outside the conference room. They were almost convinced, after standing crapping themselves before your very eyes, that you were speaking the truth and that things were going to change. All you had to do now was let them down gently, before disappearing like your predecessor (who, it turns out, left a hole the size of £12 million in company funds).

As important new and modern bosses you jot down things in your diaries that need doing to make you popular:

11 o'clock: be polite to someone useless.
1.30: think about thinking.
3.15: address some lowly member of staff by name
      (check with personnel).
5.10: ask for news of a subordinate's sick daughter
      (in front of witnesses).
7.00: smile as you leave.

At the end of the little reception to mark your enthrone-ment, Charlie had arranged a surprise for all the senior male members of the creative team: a Chewbacca dinner. So you all dressed in giant orang-utan suits before going to eat in a private room at Claridge's, where twelve hired girls did headstands naked and spread their legs so that you could eat oysters off their snatches. He's definitely got a feel for motivating the workforce, has Charlie.

31

Your first client presentation still managed to be a disaster. At Damione, Alfred Dewler and his henchman had shown the Yoplite film (the clean version) to a panel of consumers and the results of the test were not a runaway success. During the course of a raging 'conference call' you had to fight your corner against these forty-something house-wives. 'Too ethereal', 'overpromising', 'stress-inducing', 'weak product identity', 'lacking impact', 'not English enough', 'no qualitative distinction in tone and manner', 'packshot not sufficiently strong to establish identity' . . . the whole nightmare scenario. You stood your ground for the whole visio-conference, insisting that there was plenty of scope for 'modifying the soundtrack', for 'enlarging the packshot in post-production', for 'recalibrating as soon as possible', and emphasizing the importance of 'formal innovation in this niche market', of 'the susceptibility of the consumer' and 'presence in the market and in the consumer's mind', and when you hung up the client gave you an 'OK, on condition that you observe the points about reframing made in the brand review which I'll have faxed over to you ASAP.'

You find that being the boss doesn't spare you from

bowing and scraping. An art director is rather like a cabinet-maker whose client has asked for a crooked table on the pretext that he's paying for it. The advertisers don't even seem to realize it, but they're so cautious that they spend the best part of their money forcing you to make their advertisements invisible. They're so terrified of not pleasing their clients (what they would call 'altering their capital image') that they've become rigorously transparent as a result. They go through the motions of appearing on your screens but they're frightened of being noticed there. As an art director, you're only there to ratify their schizophrenia.

And so goes the great chain of contempt within advertising: the director feels only contempt for the agency, the agency feels only contempt for the advertiser, the advertiser feels only contempt for the public, and the public feel only contempt for their neighbours.

This is what's left of the thirty-second film we made for Yoplite in Miami. It's not so much a reframing as an amputation of an amputation (a stump that's been cauterized in the absence of a wooden leg?).

'Tamara in medium close-up comes and sits on the terrace of a lovely country house (**not too many clichés in the introduction before the product appears: anamorphose the actress's legs to accentuate the consumer's insight; rework her face to give her a fairer complexion**). She looks at the camera and shrieks, 'Am I beautiful? People say so. But I don't even think about it. I'm just me.' (**Get rid of 'people say so', which implies doubt, and 'but I don't even think about it', which is superfluous: if she** doesn't 'think about it' then why talk about it? Which leaves you with, 'Am I beautiful? I'm just me.') She picks up a pot of Yoplite and opens it carefully before tasting a spoonful. (**Enlarge all shots of the product.**) She closes her eyes with pleasure as she tastes the product. (**Is it possible to make this shot go on a bit longer? Let's remember that this emerged as the 'key visual' in the tests. It's crucial to dramatize the desirability of the product in order to underline the perception of a beneficial food which gives pleasure without guilt.**) Then she goes on with her script, looking the viewer straight in the eye: 'My secret is . . . Yoplite. A delicious fromage frais that's one hundred per cent fat-free. With calcium, vitamins and protein. When you want to feel good in your head and your body, there's nothing better.' (**Think about adding a 3D product demo with the fromage frais pouring unctuously into a jug with the words 'calcium', 'vitamins', 'protein' and '0 per cent fat' superimposed in bold print – more implicating/involving for the consumer**). Tamara gets up and concludes with a conspiratorial smile, 'That's my secret. But it isn't a secret now, because I've told you. Ha ha.' (**Get rid of the pointless joke, it takes up three seconds which could be put to better use on the pack-shot. We can just as easily end it on, 'That's my secret', which is more of a leader-line and is more specific in the context of the competition.**) Packshot and baseline: 'YOPLITE. KEEPS YOU IN SHAPE, MIND AND BODY.' (**Is it possible to investigate other baselines? We need to play to the different targets here: children, the elderly, adults, teenagers, men, women. And all within a very modern** framework.) Followed by the brand jingle: 'Mm, Damione'.

As far as the baseline goes, you couldn't give a stuff, because you've already got a sparc: 'YOPLITE. BECAUSE WE ALL NEED TO LIGHTEN UP SOMETIMES.' (See Act IV, Scene 26.)

32

Next it's Cannes, the festival. Oh, not the film festival, no, the other one, the real one, the one that happens on the sly, like WTO meetings and symposia in Davos, every year in June, a month after the sponsored masquerade: the International Advertising Festival or the Cannes Lions. That's where the discreet all-powerful are to be found, the people who finance feature films with their product placement (like BMW with James Bond or Peugeot with *Taxi 1* and *2*), the people who buy film studios with their pocket money (like Seagram with Universal, Sony with Columbia-triStar, AOL with Warner Bros), the people who make films only to 'support a collection' as a way of selling their merchandise (like Disney or Lucas-film), the people who own the planet (and, given that they own it, they do with it as they please). A thirty-second advertising film reaches a far wider audience than a ninety-minute feature film (the media plan for the Yoplite ad, for example, has been devised to reach 75 per cent of the population in the target countries).

All of these brands are rigorously safe from attack. They have the right to talk to you but you have no right to reply. In the press, you can say the most appalling things about human beings, but just try to knock an advertiser and you run the risk of costing your newspaper millions of pounds' worth of advertising revenue. It's even more subtle on television: there is a law to stop people naming brands on the air to avoid clandestine advertising; what this actually does is to stop people criticizing them. The brands have a right to express themselves as much as they like (and they pay heavily for this right), but *you can never answer back*. As for books . . . this novel will probably be censored for 'defamation of a registered trademark', 'plagiarizing advertising material', 'parasitism', 'libel', 'corruption' or 'unfair competition'.

At the airport the driver asks you, 'Do you have any baggage?'

You reply, 'Yes, I've got a diploma in marketing and he's got a degree in fine art.'

Charlie and you are the pinnacle of success incarnate: young, tanned, rich, terrifying, cruising up and down the Croisette in The Ross T-shirts ('We'll Ross you alive' on the front, 'At The Ross the client's the boss' on the back, some steady little employee on virtually no pay came up with the hook), your Helmut Lang Opticals sunglasses and your New Balance on your feet; you're like nabobs, but oh so cool. Logically you should be a real hit with wannabe chicks who come here to trawl for work, with their books under their arms as they wander round Jane's Club, which has been booked by some big production company who want to suck up to their creative team. For now, you're off for a free lunch on the Carlton beach with the directors of a rival production team. Every now and then you have a flash of transient pleasure, a brief moment of inexplicable happiness. You baptize these 'Near Life Experiences'.

At the buffet you recognize all the new bigshots in the trade, disguised as down-and-outs, a gang of bushy-haired (or shaven-headed), stubbly individuals in torn T-shirts, faded jeans and disintegrating trainers who draw the biggest salaries in Europe. They wear their names on badges.

There's also the Frenchman everyone calls Princess Margaret. He got this nickname because he always manages to be offered trips to Mustique by the companies he works for. Everywhere he goes people ask him how the burns on his feet have healed. It's quite funny really but, oddly enough, he doesn't seem to get the joke.

Then there are all the ageing pot-bellies, who might have had a couple of amusing ideas about twenty years ago and have been scraping a living off them ever since. One of them built a personal fortune by selling the same slogan to all his different clients: 'If you want coffee, you want Gold Blend', 'If you want bleach, you want Domestos', 'If you want tissues, you want Kleenex', 'If you want butter, you want Lurpak' . . . You all make a tremendous effort to look as if you're enjoying yourselves. Enjoying yourself is like committing suicide, except you can do it every day. As soon as anyone mentions Browning in front of you and Charlie, you affect the appropriately devastated expression: 'Oh dear, oh dear, oh dear, please don't talk about him, we miss him so much. D'you know we still get mail for him, ImageBank catalogues addressed to him. Christ, they could update their database, for fuck's sake. The whole profession's in mourning. Anyway, Cannes's had it . . . Shall we meet up at the Martinez bar this evening after the short-list?'

The short-list is the jury's selection of the 100 best advertising films (out of 500 candidates). And you're on it with your 'Yoplite, it's so good when it comes in your mouth'. The jury, made up of British, French, Japanese, German, American and Brazilian colleagues, thought it was so risqué that it was worth short-listing, despite some booing and hissing in the auditorium. You scraped in with the Dogma version at the last minute, having aired it just once at three o'clock in the morning on an obscure cable channel. It could, therefore, legally be considered to be a real campaign, even though the client didn't want anything to do with it and the public had never seen it (on the other hand the 'cauterized stump' version is on maximum rotation on ITV every evening with its new baseline, 'YOPLITE. BECAUSE WE ALL NEED TO LIGHTEN UP SOMETIMES', but it goes without saying that it didn't get past the first round here). Tamara should be joining you tomorrow. It really would be fantastic to win a prize barely a month after being appointed as head of Rosserys & Crow London. There you would be, stepping up on to the stage, getting mentions on television and in the press: 'Britain, at the cutting edge of creativity in advertising, has carried away a Golden Lion at the International Advertising Festival in Cannes for Damione's Yoplite, with its pastiche of a pornographic film from the Rosserys & Crow agency, which has just appointed two joint art directors.' There'd be a picture of you in *Campaign* with a caption something like this: 'Octave Parengo and Charlie Nargood announce, "*We must federate all this enthusiasm and channel it into the creative process of tomorrow.*"'

A few words picked up on the water-ski pontoon of the Majestic Hotel, from various people slapping each other's hands in hearty greeting:

'I'm bored of Dior.'

'Have you seen the new thirty-second film with the rabbit bungee-jumping?'

'And the one for the Renault Mégane where the brakes make everyone's hair go weird?'

'Fan-tastic. Fan-fucking-tastic.'

'The new British Airways is perfect.'

'I'm not so convinced by the new Diesel. It's a bit laboured.'

'The Tag Heuer campaign is pants.'

'Yeah, but the latest Pepsi series was fucking brilliant.'

'What d'you think about Radio 1, with the big black guy singing in the Beetle?'

'Telmor have gone over the top.'

'The Norwegians are going to clean up again.'

'There's going to be a standing ovation for the gay who gets picked up by the girl.'

'It's a hell of an idea.'

'Have you seen the two blokes in the sauna? You can smell the money from here.'

'I love your Yoplite, but it's too bad there are no animals in it. Cats and dogs are very Cannes.'

'Did you know that our fathers were very nearly associates?'

'Really? Give me a kiss, then. What's your name?'

'Nathalie Lightfoot.'

'Yes, you know, I'm the one who likes to be cheeky . . .'

Screwed-up smile.

'I'm going to tell you something. If you're not with me, you're against me.'

'Oh! I thought you were serious!'

'No, I've had enough now. I make sure I'm in the southern hemisphere in winter.'

'Have you seen our little Yoplite?'

'Überfashion.'

'I love the idea but not the execution.'

'No, but seriously, do you like it or don't you?'

'If I had to choose between "I like it" and "I don't like it", it would have to be "I don't like it"'.

'Stop it. I'm immuno-depressed.'

'No, I'm teasing. Frankly, I think it's great, but I'm not sure how the baseline's going to work for everyone because of the play on words.'

'Yeah, but the Americans are such puritans that they'll all vote for it. As soon as there's something a bit raunchy they think it's incredibly risqué cos they couldn't possibly come up with something like that themselves.'

Thumbs up.

'The other day I was in a meeting and a client came out with, "It's good, but you need to add some today-ness."

D'you know what I asked him? "And would you like some tomorrow-tude as well?" '

Vaginal laugh.

'I've got a group leader who keeps talking about "gustatoriness"! He doesn't even know the word "taste"!'

'You don't learn about taste in business school.'

'Anyway, it's always better to say "I just adore you" than "I can't stand the sight of you." '

'The absolutely best one is the one with the bloke singing "Get up . . . ah" while he waits for the car which goes past every day.'

'Haven't seen it. Will you have the tape sent round?'

'It's really right for the product but at the same time totally true to the idea.'

'It's mucho ethereal.'

'Yeah, but it's also mucho macho.'

'I can't believe Nike've been short-listed now that we've heard the testimonial from Hulk's wife.'

'It must be because the Japanese didn't take any of it on board.'

'That Yoplite porno, though, you had to have the balls.'

'It's so simple, it works like a dream.'

'It's gonna slaughter them.'

'Have you heard about Tony Kaye's latest? He insisted on having a tunnel built with 600 sea breams nailed to the walls, and then he never used it.'

'I'm launching a new form of media, I just have to tell you about it. It's called a "magalogue": it's halfway between a magazine and a catalogue.'

'Why don't you call it a catazine?'

Eyes to the heavens.

'How's Sophie?'

'She's expecting a baby.'

'Well I never! How funny, I'm expecting some cocktail nibbles any minute.'

'E-hi, there.'

That's Matthew Cocteau, who used to work as a copywriter and who's moved into designing Internet sites.

'E-hello. So, are things going well for your little e-business?'

'E-yup. I earned myself e-20 million in e-six months.'

'Well what the e-hell are you doing @ here.com?'

'We need e-you. We need some advertising to publicize my schmucky little sites and they need advertising in them, too, so that we can finance them by selling ad space on the screen. This new economy isn't new at all. Just like the old one. It only survives on advertising.'

'Let me tell you, our greatest feat, having turned the public right off advertising in the eighties, was to convince them that we'd gone out of fashion in the nineties and had been overtaken by the Net in the new millennium. When, in fact, we've never been so powerful!'

'E-right. Not too much e-time to e-chat with you. Gotta go to the cybercafé on the beach to check my mails. Okay, e-ciao.'

'Bye-bye.com!'

And that night in the Nibarland, you dance sitting down in your chairs. It's a fashion that's come over from New York. The mayor there has clamped down so heavily on licences for nightclubs that all the people who want to party flock to bars where there's no dancing. In Spy, Velvet, Jet, Chaos, Liquid and Life they listen to excruciatingly loud hip hop music and make do with waggling their arms without ever getting up off their stools. And now the trend's come over the Atlantic. It's the height of uncool to throw yourself about on a dance floor. All over the world, it's now crucial to remain seated amid the general cacophony if you want to be where it's at. In the disco in Cannes you can quickly tell who lives here all year round, because they're dancing with the pretty local girls and having a whale of a time, while all the ad execs sit on their velour banquettes sipping drinks to show their colleagues that they've just come back from New York City. And you, Charlie and you, you make a point of getting up from the table ten times to go to the Gents, waiting there for five minutes and coming back with your hair in a mess, sniffing and drinking great quantities of water while you scratch your noses, just to make the Japanese think that you've got some coke when they haven't.

This time it feels as if you're in a David Lynch film. Beneath the smiling, refined exterior lies a darker dimension, a secret violence, a destructive madness which forces you to smile all the wider.

33

And now slip, if you will, into the skin of the fifty-three-year-old Police Commissioner Sanchez Ferlosio, in his narrow little office in downtown Cannes. It's the end of the day, you can feel the weekend creeping up peacefully, you can hear the cicadas chirping and you can just imagine the glass of white wine on the bar at the Buffet de la Gare, when suddenly, something happens. You receive an international arrest warrant by e-mail with an attachment in RealVideo. You double-click on the icon and you find yourself looking at black-and-white images of three people coming out of a villa yelling, 'D'you think it's recording?', 'No, it's just an intercom', 'Anyway, even if they tried to trace us, no one knows us here', before coming right up to the lens with big stones in their hands.

You laboriously decipher a message in English headed 'First-degree Murder Inquiry'. Your English isn't very good but, basically, it seems that the Miami branch of the Florida police are investigating people granted licences to film on location in February. The name of the three British suspects scroll before your eyes and, when you see their professions, you quickly understand why you're getting dragged into this: you, here and now, right in the middle of the International Festival of Advertising. You think wistfully of the days when your job was slow and boring; and you pick up your telephone to get hold of a list of people booked into the various Palaces along the Croisette.

You and Tamara wake up as the day is going to bed. The curtains at the Carlton are very thick and you only have to put the 'Do not disturb' sign on your door handle to be left in peace by the cleaners for the whole day. You drank yourself into oblivion all night but you still haven't gone back to coke. You preferred to experiment with some mushrooms someone had brought back from a smart-shop in Amsterdam. Thanks to them, at about four o'clock in the morning, you came up with an idea for an ad for Lemvix capsules.

'A blonde with neatly blow-dried hair is sitting in the back of a huge Mercedes with a rich Arab. The chauffeur has a very bad cold. He suddenly starts working up to a dramatic sneeze – "Ahh. . . . ahh . . ." just as the car is diving into the Alma tunnel. Black screen. There's a screech of brakes and the terrible sound of a violent impact. The Lemvix logo appears with the following baseline: "LEMVIX CAPSULES. STOP YOUR COLD BEFORE IT STOPS YOU DEAD".'

Not bad, you think to yourself as you read back your idea from the tablecloth where you scribbled it. You could invoice thousands for something like that. But there's better.

'John Kennedy is flying a private jet over Long Island. He has a very bad cold, and keeps coughing and sneezing. His wife, Carolyn, is a little worried – no, beset with worries . . . get it? (Her maiden name's Bessette.) She offers him a Lemvix capsule but John won't take it because they're running very late to get to his cousin's wedding. He suddenly starts sneezing violently, veering the plane off course. The Lemvix logo appears with the following baseline: "LEMVIX. WHEN YOU DON'T WANT TO NOSE-DIVE".'

Yesterday evening you made love for the first time and it was wonderful, fruitily and logically wonderful. Octave, you deserve your reputation as an expert on the art of penetration. On MTV, REM were singing 'It's the end of the world and I feel fine'. Tamara came over to you. You were looking for a napkin to wipe your fingers, which were all greasy because you'd just eaten an apricot doughnut. She started it by licking your fingers; then the rest. You joined in, or you both joined each other, hard to tell the difference. Her lips were sugary (the apricot doughnut). She stroked you with her long hair. Tamara's skin gleamed so much you could see your reflection in it. You had a second hard-on straight after you'd come. And that's something that hadn't happened to you for a long time. When you live with someone, the second erection doesn't happen any more. You don't lay the table again straight after a meal. And yet it's so good: you've just ejaculated, you look at each other, drink a bit of water, smoke a cigarette and suddenly, bang, in just one look, the urge is there again, you're pussy's dripping again and your prick's hurting it's so hard. Baseline: 'FEELING THE STRAIN? TAMARA GETS YOU UP AGAIN!'

While she slept, beads of sweat appeared like dew on her shoulders and forehead. It reminded you of a book you'd read somewhere about Creole women 'sleeping so gracefully, with all the indolence of those who never do anything'. You still can't believe it took you so long to get around to taking off her little white top. If only you'd known it was going to be so good . . . There she was last night, Tamara eating an anagram of herself, taramasalata, by the pool of the Majestic Hotel, and she said, 'Do you want me to have you?'

'Hey! Your tits are pointing at me!'

'Yup, point and shoot, that's what I usually do.'

When she turned her head she turned men's heads. Her hair glowed gold, her profile gleamed like honey, her tawny eyes sparkled – every part of her you looked at turned to gold. Her hair looked as if it had been left behind, as if it had trouble following her as it floated behind her, wafting the smoky air with a perfume you recognized: Obsession . . . Sophie's perfume, from the early days, when she was testing out her power over you by pouting with her mouth tantalizingly half open, like an ad campaign for a new range of lipsticks from L'Oréal. But thinking about Sophie reminds you that you fucked without a condom.

'Watch out, Tamara. I'm extremely fertile.'

'Oh, what a crisis. I've been on the pill for ten years. I hope you haven't got anything, though.'

You both pretend to sleep in front of cable TV. You're woken up by Charlie yelling down the phone, 'We've got AIDS! We've got AIDS!'

'What?'

'It's happened. The Department of Health has just appointed us to manage their campaign for preventing the spread of AIDS. Isn't that fantastic? It's £5 million and no competition!'

Tamara turns towards you. 'What is it?'

'Oh, nothing . . . It was Charlie . . . We've got AIDS.'

The previous morning you ingested the hallucinogenic mushrooms from Amsterdam, psilocybes (four heads and three stems each), and your conversation took a new turn.

'You've got two heads.'

'The cupboard's going to explode.'

'Christ, what a fix!'

'I want to watch a film but I don't know why. Is that normal?'

'By the time I understand what you're asking it's too late to reply.'

'I can't stop my head spinning. It's going round and round.'

'I've just had a fight with the mini-bar.'

'Sticks and stones won't break my bones but names will always hurt me.'

'I'm coming back to myself.'

'I don't feel like watching some tits and ass thing, but I'm going to anyway.'

'Trouble with you girls is we have to find reasons for you to keep us.'

'I can't stand sentences that begin with 'I can't stand'.'

'You quench my thirst.'

'You never stop cheating on me.'

'Yup, but I could have done worse. I could have married you.'

Do you know the difference between the rich and the poor? The poor sell drugs so that they can buy Nikes whereas the rich sell Nikes so that they can buy drugs.

The sea danced along the dark margin of the gulf. The sea never changed, never altered. It was only the following morning that Tamara announced she was leaving and she wouldn't be coming back.

'Who with?'

'Alfred Dewler, your client from Damione! He's crazy about me. He leaves twenty messages a day on my voice-mail. We slept together last week. He took me to the Savoy. He couldn't believe it was happening to him. He was scared to death. It was rather sweet. He's pretty nice really, you know. He made all sorts of declarations of love to me. I think he really wants to leave his wife, you know. He's bored with his life.'

'Oh, that isn't a scoop. He also bores millions of other people. But what are you going to do about your daughter. Will you leave her in Morocco?'

'No, no, Alfred's quite happy to get British citizenship for her. He wants us to set up house together. He's going to ask for a divorce. He wants us to get married, the works . . . You know, it's amazing what a mess you can make of a middle-aged man's life when you have a slim waist and an agile tongue . . .'

'Yeah, and you're twenty years younger than his wife.'

'Look, don't sulk. You know I'm not going to get many opportunities like this. It's the chance of a lifetime! I'm going to be able to settle down to become a real middle-class housewife. I'll have a house of my own for the first time. I'll be able to decorate it, and I'll be called Mrs Dewler, and my daughter will be Miss Dewler, and we'll have a car and holidays abroad. I'll have some security, and I'll be able to put on some weight at last! But I'm not going to forget you. You will come to the party, won't you? I'd even like you to be one of our witnesses, but Alfred said no. He's very jealous of my past.'

'Have you told him everything? Watch out. He is my biggest client after all.'

'Um . . . no, not all the details. Anyway, he doesn't really want to hear them, but, well, he's guessed that we've been fooling around together.'

'Which was not true until last night.'

'Yes, that's why I raped you. It bugged me that we'd never actually done it. Hey, you were on good form. It was great. Did you like it? I didn't want to leave you till you'd had a taste of the goods. It's only thanks to you that all this is happening to me . . .' As she says this she points to the cover of *Elle* magazine, a photo of herself smiling taken by Corinne Day with the caption 'Tamara: Yoplite's Moorish delight'.

'But don't you want to come to the Lions award ceremony?'

'Listen, Alfred doesn't really want to. He's very posses-sive. I don't want to upset him. Especially because he's right. He says that if I want a career in cinema, I shouldn't be cheapening myself with advertising any more.'

'So this is the end, is it? And just when I was beginning to love you!'

'Stop. Last time you said that to me it was too soon, and now it's too late.'

And that's it, she kisses you one last time and you let her slender wrists slip from your grasp. You let her go because you let everyone go. You let her slip away to the superstar career that you all know so well. You feel more and more tubercular. The second she closes the door, nostalgia for all the seconds before engulfs you.

The sky melts into the sea; it's known as the horizon. 'In the dawn of the third millennium . . .' People have been talking about it for such a long time it feels strange to be a part of it, 'the dawn of the new millennium' – not all it was cracked up to be. There are petrol tankers crossing the bay and the sea in their wake is iridescent (polluted, in other words). You look at Sophie's scan. It's becoming hazy, but you don't blink. You keep your eyes wide open until your cheeks are soaked.

You meet people who come and transform your life without knowing it and then they betray you. Softly, softly, they betray you. You see them making their pacts with the enemy, and then you watch them leave, like an army retreating after pillaging a town. You watch them leave against a background of rubble and the setting sun.

34

You are the products of an age. No, why the age? You are products, full stop. Because globalization is no longer interested in people, you had to become products before society would take any interest in you. Capitalism transforms people into perishable yoghurts, addicted to shows – in other words, trained to wipe out those around them. To get yourself fired all you'd have to do would be to drag your name across the screen to Trash and then to select 'Empty Trash' on the 'Special' menu. The computer would ask, 'Are you sure you want to empty Trash? Cancel. OK.' To magic yourself away, you'd just have to click on 'OK'. They used to say 'Clunk click every trip', and that little click of your seat belt was meant to save your life in a crash, but now just one little click of the mouse could mean the biggest crash of all for you.

Given that you are a product, you'd like to have a complicated, unpronounceable name that no one can remember, the name of a shit-coloured hard drug, a really powerful acid that can dissolve a tooth in just an hour, an over-sugared liquid with a strange taste which, despite all its obvious faults, is still the most widely recognized brand on earth. You'd like to be a fizzy drink.

In the meantime, if you were Charlie Nargood in his hotel room, you'd be surfing on various sexual websites and you'd be very happy to download an 'entertaining' (as you still insist on calling them) video, showing a young Asian girl sucking off a horse before spewing up a litre of its spunk, and that reminds you that it's high time you went and made yourself beautiful for the global Lions award ceremony. Only there'd be a problem. Olivia, who would no longer be a trainee but a recently promoted senior art director, would have been in the bathroom for the last forty-five minutes.

And if you were Octave Parengo, you'd be outside the Palais des Festivals (you know, the neo-Nazi-inspired blockhouse at the end of the Croisette, where the stars go up the red staircase at Cannes to a strobe effect of flashing cameras). You'd be hanging around in a crowd of ad execs from all over the world, all in their hired dinner suits and all getting ready for the giving out of self-congratulatory trophies. You would hear the hubbub of the crowd, you would smell the intoxicating perfumes and rank sweat of terror. You would contemplate the beach, its fine sand, its white yachts. If you look behind you it's at some fat foreign git standing too close – it's not at 2,000 years of history. You would look back towards the 50,000-year-old sand which couldn't give a flying fuck about you. What's 2,000 years compared to sand? Because you were born just before the turn of the millennium, there's no need to make such a meal of it.

You know you'll come out of this all right. You just need an idea. You'll always find something to get you back on the scene: selling people porn films in which they make love with their own parents (reconstituted with synthesized pictures), parachuting fat-free yoghurt drinks into starving countries, launching a drug in suppository form, or a suppository in the form of a dildo, suggesting to Coca-Cola that they should dye their drink red to save on labelling costs, telling the President of the United States that he should bomb Iraq every time he has problems with internal politics, suggesting to Calvin Klein that they should launch a range of genetically modified foodstuffs, to Damione that they should design bio-active clothes, to Bill Gates that he should buy up all the poor countries, to Nutella that they should make a hazlenut-flavoured soap, to Lacoste that they should mass-market vacuum-packed crocodile meat, to Pepsi-Cola that they should inaugurate their own blue television channel, to the Esso group that they should open a chain of knocking shops at all their service stations, to Gillette that they should launch an eight-blade razor . . . You'll come out of this all right, won't you?

What the hell, into the fray!

35

The auditorium is full to bursting. Your heart's beating like a drum. You run your hands through your hair and you spray breath-freshener in your mouth. Your hour of glory is here. You're a bit pissed off with Tamara for giving you the slip, but it doesn't matter, Olivia's French-kissing with Charlie, there are 6,000 people in the auditorium and you may be going to step up on to the stage if you win an award . . . Everything's fine. So why does your smile feel more and more fixed?

You engage the woman on your left in conversation .

'Bonjour. My name is Charlie and this is Octave.'

'I know. You're the new bosses at The Ross.'

'Oh, I'm in luck, you speak English. And where do you work?'

'At The Ross. Amanda, I work in production.'

'Ah, yes, of course, Amanda. Now I recognize you. I'm so sorry. We've hardly slept for three days.'

'No problem. Do you think the Yoplite film is in with a chance?'

'Hard to tell. Possibly. It's so stupid that it could get through.'

'Oh, by the way, I was meant to tell you. Lady Di and John-John are going off to be tested.'

'I know, I know. And we've got AIDs.'

'Yes. I'm in the picture. We're already in full-speed-ahead mode on that.'

The lights dim. Hearty applause. You cross your legs, you look at your watch, you wait for your category (Milk & Dairy Products) as you tidy your hair with your fingers. Before your eyes the most creative advertising films on the planet unfurl: wild flights of fancy about cornflakes, weight-loss diets, perfumes, jeans, shampoos, vodka, chocolate bars, noodles, pizzas, computers, free Internet sites, dog food, four-wheel drives, flashes of imagination and self-mockery which miraculously escaped the advertisers' vigilance, innovative typefaces, soft-focus shots of green apples, grainy images shot in 16mm, designs of tomorrow, catchphrases, 3D red logos, Hindu animations, double double-bluffs, parodies of well-known tunes, extremes of everything, bullet points, money spent, film scratched by hand frame by frame, crowds shot in slow motion, emotions unleashed, and always pretty girls, because everything comes back to pretty girls, people aren't interested in anything else. You try to give an impression of nonchalance to your neighbour, who keeps wriggling in her seat and is humming to herself to try to appear relaxed. If this scene had taken place before all that sexual revolution business in the 1960s (but it couldn't have happened before then because it is a consequence of that time) it would have been recognized as the trigger, the turning point, the defining moment of the onset of free love.

'And the winner is. . . . Yoplite – The Nymphomaniac, by Rosserys & Crow London!'

Glory be to Thee, Golden Lion. Hosanna in the highest. For Thine is the kingdom, the power and the glory, for ever and ever, Amen.

You explode with joy,

'Yyyyyyessssssss!',

go down past the rows of seats,

go up the steps to the stage,

and you get ready to thank the director, Enrique, 'without whom we wouldn't be here', and the beautiful Tamara, 'thanks to whom all this was possible', and to say that your idea was to 'sing a hymn to life which respected human timing'

and everything that goes with it,

when suddenly they're upon you.

Three policemen nab you in front of representatives of your profession from all over the world, and it's Police Commissioner Sanchez Ferlosio himself who handcuffs you for the murder of Mrs Ward of Coral Gables, District of Miami, State of Florida.

In a way, you could say that you put yourself out of contention.

36

'Life is like this: you're born, you die, and in between you have stomach ache. To live is to have stomach ache, the whole time. At fifteen your stomach aches because you're in love; at twenty-five because you're worried about the future; at thirty-five because you drink; at forty-five because you work too hard; at fifty-five because you're not in love any more; at sixty-five because you're worried about the past; at seventy-five because you're riddled with cancer. In between all you will have done is to obey your parents, then the teachers, then the bosses, then the husbands, then the doctors. Sometimes you'll wonder whether they really give a fuck about you, but it's already too late, and one day one of them tells you you're going to die and then you're tidied away into a wooden box on a rainy day, and put under ground in a cemetery somewhere in the suburbs. You think you've been spared? Bully for you. When you read this, I'll be dead. You'll be alive and I won't. Isn't that devastating? You'll be walking about, drinking, eating, fucking, you'll have a choice, but I, I won't be doing any of those things. I'll be somewhere else, in a place I don't know any more than you do, but which I will know by the time you come to read these lines. Death lies between us. It's not sad, it's just that – me being dead and you reading this letter – we are on either side of an insurmountable wall and yet we can still talk to each other. To live and to hear a corpse speaking to you: clever, the Internet, isn't it!

Your favourite ghost,

Sophie.'

You just stand staring at each other, you and Sophie's parents; as if you would be able to speak in this visiting room now that Sophie's no longer here, when you never could while she was alive. They've ended up visiting you in Wandsworth jail: you, Octave, the rotten apple they used to avoid at family gatherings. Their eyes are swollen with great dark rings under them. Four huge, red, despairing marbles.

'She sent this message by e-mail from a hotel in Senegal. Have you heard anything from her since . . .'

'Since we split up? No. And it's not for lack of trying.'

The evidence hits you like a physical blow. She was in Senegal when Browning committed suicide . . . Did they do themselves in together? What the hell was she doing there with him? Fuck, it's bad enough finding out you've been cheated on, but if you find out posthumously and when you're in the nick . . .

'It's not possible. It can't be true. It can't be true. It's not possible.' (You alternate between these two sentences for an hour, precious little point in transcribing your lamentations here.)

You look at them, the old couple with the trembling

chins. Just after leaving the visiting room you dissolve into tears in front of a magazine ad for Freedom Air. It's not the first time you've blubbed since your incarceration. In fact, for a couple of hard nuts, you cry quite a lot, you and Charlie. So much so that he tried to hang himself the day after he arrived here. And you wail, 'I didn't love her any more but I'd still love her except that I didn't love her enough when I loved her since for ever without loving her as I should have loved her.'

You're still crying as you write these lines.

Bergson described laughter as 'mechanics stuck on to living matter'. Tears must, therefore, be the opposite: living matter stuck on to mechanics. A robot breaking down, a dandy succumbing to unaffectedness, an insurrection of truth in the midst of all this artifice. Suddenly a stranger jabs you in the guts with his fork. Suddenly a psycopath buggers you in the showers. Suddenly a stranger tells you goodbye with an ultrasound scan. When a pregnant woman commits suicide, that's two dead for the price of one, like a special offer on soap powder. Even the songs on the radio seem to be there to taunt you: 'Killing me softly with her e-mail, telling my whole life with her words, killing me softly with her e-mail, killing me softly . . .'

one last ad break, and see you back in a minute.

A man sits alone on the floor in an unfurnished apartment.

Slow-motion black-and-white flashback: The bailiffs coming and taking all his possessions, a row with his wife, who leaves, slamming the door behind her. We know that he has nothing left.

Back to him. He's gazing despairingly at the camera.

A voice (off) addresses him sharply: 'Has your wife left you? Have you run out of money? Are you ugly and thick? All that can be changed in the twinkling of an eye.'

The man is interested in this voice. He nods his head. Then he suddenly pulls a gun out of his pocket and points it at his temple.

The voice-over goes on: 'Dying sets you free, as free as you were before you were born.'

The man shoots himself in the head. His skull explodes. His brain is splattered over the walls. But he's not completely dead. He lies on the floor shivering, his face covered in blood. The camera moves up to his mouth. He whispers: 'Thank you, death.'

He stops moving, his eyes wide open, staring at the ceiling.

The voice-over concludes conspiratorially: 'Make death your closest ally. Suicide puts an end to life and all the years of heartache and strife!'

BASELINE WITH BFPS LOGO: 'Wave your worries goodbye when you choose to die.'

FOLLOWED BY THE LEGAL NOTICE: 'This message was brought to you by the British Federation for a Peaceful Suicide (BFPS).'

Other possible baselines:

£6.99

'Death – it's deadly fashionable.'
'Can't get a life? Get dead instead.'
'Life? Leave it to your friends.'

6 They

'I live in so many cities. I don't know who I am. I live in the future. I miss the present.'

Tom Ford

37

They're not dead. They're on an island. They breath the air and frolic in the sun. Mark Browning and Sophie look ridiculous and they couldn't care less. Put it down to happiness, that's whose fault it is. They live in the water. They end up loving each other. If you make love all that often, you end up putting some feeling into it. They left Senegal for a little hut with no TV or radio or disco or air-conditioning or cans of beer or anything but themselves. They grill the fish that the local fishermen catch and eat it with coconut rice, pickling themselves on punch under the white clouds. In Senegal they didn't come across anyone on the beach except for a kind American. They're very well, thank you, they've run away, they've won. They're laughing quietly to themselves. It was the American who killed them.

Young vandals who go round setting cars alight understand everything about our society. They don't burn them because they can't have them; they burn them so as not to want them.

They're so cute. Mark and Sophie . . . they deserve each other.

Ghost Island in the archipelago of the Cayman Islands.

How did they end up over there? The American's name was Mike, but his name doesn't matter. It was probably a false identity anyway. With his craggy face he looked like the photographer Peter Beard. He introduced himself as a retired former FBI agent. They chatted with him on the beach of the Savana Hotel complex at Saly. After a few drinks, they explained their situation to him: Mark's embezzling, his imminent redundancy, Sophie's pregnancy, the fact that they wanted to get away from it all. Mike offered them a deal: to disappear for ever. To fake their own deaths in order to disappear. He knew the procedure well, having used it for years when he ran the FBI's rehabilitation programme for 'repentant' Mafiosi. His entire professional experience had consisted of hiding former criminals, having their faces redesigned, changing their identities and sending them to a location which would remain a closely guarded secret. And now he'd found a little trick for making ends meet more than handsomely: giving certain individuals an opportunity to benefit from his skills. He made only one condition: they must never come back. To kill Mark and Sophie, all he needed was a mini Polaroid camera, two real United States passports and a load of official stamps . . . and that's how Mark and Sophie became Patrick and Caroline Burnham.

There comes a point, if you keep telling people that their lives are futile, when they all go completely mad, they run around screaming, they can't accept the fact that their existence has no meaning, no goal. When you think about it, it's difficult to conceive that we're here for nothing, just to die. Hardly surprising that everyone on earth goes barking.

What exactly is happiness? It's white sand, blue sky, salty water. An ad for a Thompson's holiday, in other words. Happiness is to step inside a Thompson's poster, or Ambre Solaire with the long-limbed smiling women and the blond smiling children. Mark and Sophie used to make advertisements; now Patrick and Caroline have become one. They've chosen to end their life in one of their creations, like tanned stereotypes, a cover for *Hello!*, a Yoplite campaign with the teak veranda and an exotic background, a Sandals ad with its pretty typeface and sun-drenched views.

38

Script:

Patrick is still young and good-looking. He's steering a speedboat over the sea. The role could be played by Mark Browning. He jumps out of the moving boat and swims towards the beach. A gorgeous woman walks over to him. She has a beautiful smiling baby in her arms. He runs up to her. Moving music by Ennio Morricone. The role of the woman could be played by Sophie, Octave's ex. They hug each other, raising their child towards the perfect sky. Just then a seaplane flies over them. Reverse-angle shot of their faces as they open their eyes wide with amazement. The baby bursts out laughing. Back to the plane, which turns out to be a tanker plane, and it becomes clear why their faces have lit up. The plane is banking round and dropping fifty tonnes of multicoloured confetti. The music swells (sound to maximum in post-prod). Slow-motion travelling shot drawing away from them along the beach, followed by sequence shot swooping past them. Viewers should weep every tear in their bodies as they watch this instant of pure beauty: The united couple, the perfect setting, the innocent baby and the rain of red, blue, yellow, green and white confetti. They are clearly on a desert island, surrounded by coconut palms and white sand.

Baseline (CHOICE OF):

Happiness puts an end to sorrow.

When happiness calls sadness falls.

Happiness doesn't belong to Nestlé.

Happiness is as good as it gets.

39

God, they're so perfect. In love, on their private desert island in the Caymans. Ghost Island doesn't appear on any geographical map. The days there are spent watching the sky and the sea and a child who smiles as she watches the sky and the sea. The trees aren't branded: there isn't a 'coconut' logo on them. Caroline and Patrick have found a way out – listening to the silence, preferably while lying in a hammock.

'It's not me who's looking after my daughter,' says Caroline, *'It's my daughter who's looking after me.'*

They trust this world because they believe they've escaped it. The things of this world are not as strong as the life of this world. At last they know what it is to love. They look at their daughter, look at each other, then look at her again, and so on, indefinitely. The baby watches the pelicans. That's all they do for hours, days, weeks. Enough to give you a hell of a stiff neck, and anyone who hasn't experienced that deserves sympathy all round.

'I left because I couldn't believe there was more.'
'What did you say?'
'I left because I couldn't breathe any more.'
Somewhere over the Caribbean waters between Cuba

and Honduras, God sprinkled the Cayman Islands. You can land there only in a light aircraft. The runway at Little Cayman Airport crosses the island's one and only road. The village numbers 110 inhabitants, excluding iguanas. In Grand Cayman there are some 600 financial establishments with numbered accounts. The Caymans are a British colony with their own independent government and 35,000 off-shore businesses on their trade registers. To get to Ghost Island you have to take a secret canoe-taxi (Mike went with them).

They'll feel great there. Actually, they already smell great: coconut, vanilla rum, honey, spices, sea air, Calvin Klein's Obsession, ganja and rain in the early evenings. Wafting scents to delight every sense.

'I'm drinking your mouth, licking your teeth, sucking your tongue. I'm sipping your sighs, swallowing your cries.'

For £1 million in cash, Mike arranged everything: the repatriation of the fake ashes, Sophie's farewell e-mail, the transfer of funds to Switzerland . . . He was quite used to sending his clients to the Castaneda Escape Complex, a hotel where the weather's beautiful all year round. A group of bungalows built of rosewood, beefwood and teak, hidden in a forest of hibiscus and frangipani.

They've set up home in a little reed hut, a straw hut on stilts over a cerulean lagoon. Every evening they meet the other fake-dead of the island: Kirsty McColl (forty-one) and Elvis Presley (sixty-eight) listen as little Kurt Cobain (thirty-six) composes country music songs with Jimi Hendrix (fifty-nine); one former leader of the labour party, John Smith (sixty-four), chats to another, Harold Wilson (eighty-six); Mike Hutchens (forty-two) strolls hand in hand with Paula Yates (forty-two); Eric Morecambe (seventy-six) and Peter Sellers (seventy-seven) are setting up a practical joke for everyone on the beach; John-John Kennedy (forty-three) walks about arm in arm with his father John Fitzgerald Kennedy (eighty-six) and the actress Marilyn Monroe (seventy-five).

While the gentle breeze turns the palm trees into giant fans, Patrick and Caroline sip orangeade with John Lennon (sixty-two), who lives on the other side of the island in a bamboo hut with Klaus Kinski (seventy-seven) and Charles Bukowski (eighty-two). One of the co-founders of the Escape Complex which bears his name, the psyche-delic writer Carlos Castaneda (about sixty-three) takes his peyote mushrooms with Sylvia Plath (seventy-one) as he casts an eye over Ghost Island's capital gains on the stock market. The secret island in fact finances itself on the interest from the capital put in by all its inhabitants (the entry ticket being fixed at $3 million). A team of transgenic doctors and bionic surgeons manage to prolong the existence of all these islanders to the age of about 120. All the inhabitants of Ghost are officially dead in the eyes of the world (with only two exceptions: Paul McCartney and Salman Rushdie have been living on Ghost Island for ten years and have been replaced by lookalikes in the 'real world'), but that's no reason to let yourself go. Plastic surgery, skin grafts, face-lifts, implants and silicone injections are all free, like everything else for that matter. That's why Grace Kelly doesn't look anything like her seventy-three years as she talks shop with Bing Crosby (ninety-eight) and Frank Sinatra (eighty-five), her co-stars from *High Society*.

Diana Spencer and Dodi Al-Fayed are there too, aged forty-two and forty-eight respectively.

They while away a peaceful existence in this billionaires' retirement home where television, telephones, the Internet and all other forms of communication are strictly forbidden. Only books and digital disks are authorized. Every month the plasma screens installed in the bungalows automatically have the 10,000 key new events in literature, music and film downloaded on to them from the outside world. Child prostitutes of both sexes (hired by the year) mean that each of the islanders can satisfy their every erotic desire.

Yes, if you stop to think about it, what they want to make us believe – to accept that there isn't anything else and that we're just here by chance – is almost as barmy as saddling us with a bearded God surrounded by angels. And the Flood, Noah's Ark and Adam and Eve are as preposterous to believe in as the Big Bang and the dinosaurs.

Patrick and Caroline sip their drinks by the turquoise sea. They're drinking pineapple juice under the hanging mangroves while butterflies the size of your hand flit around them. Every drug known to man is dropped off on their doormat every morning in a dinky Hermès suitcase. But they don't always take them; they sometimes even go several days without shooting up, or having an orgy, or torturing the slaves. Caroline gave birth in the ultra-modern clinic on Ghost Island, known as the Hemingway Hospital (a nod to the American writer's false death in Kenya in 1954).

Soon countries will be replaced by companies. We will no longer be citizens of nations, we will live in brands: you could be from Microsoftia or McDonaldland; you could be Calvin Kleinish or Pradan.

They wear ecru linen. They have been relieved of the problem of death and, therefore, of time too. They're no longer answerable to anyone in the rest of the world. They are like apprentices to freedom, as Jesus Christ was when he rose out of his tomb three days after his tormented death and had to yield to the evidence. Even death is transient, only paradise lasts a long time. They watch their daughter babbling with her nanny. She keeps an eye on the monkeys and is totally unimpressed with the peacocks. Caroline is beautiful, so Patrick is happy. Patrick is happy, so Caroline is beautiful. An eternity set to the rhythm of the surf. They sit between the exotic trees that glow red and gold in the sunset, eating delicious grilled fish, deep-fried cod balls and lobster with vanilla. Their only clothes? Open shirts over surfing shorts. Their chief concern? Not burning the soles of their feet too much on the white sand. Their present preoccupation? Having a shower to get the salt off their skin. Their only anxiety? Being careful when they swim because there are currents that could carry them out to sea and kill them for real.

40

When they went into the dock, the presiding judge asked everyone else to be seated and Charlie and Octave to stand up, but they just lowered their heads. The duty policemen took off their handcuffs. It was like being in a church: the rituals, the solemn rites, the robes – there's not much difference between a law court and a church service. With one exception: they wouldn't be granted forgiveness. Octave and Charlie were not proud of themselves, but they were happy that Tamara had managed to get out of it. It was a public trial, and every representative of their profession seemed to be there in the courtroom – the same ones who had been to Browning's funeral. From the dock they could see them all, and they could see that everything was going to go on without them. They got ten years, but they can't really complain (luckily they were tried in England and the British authorities refused to extradite them: if they'd been tried in America they would have been grilled like sausages on a barbecue in a Herta ad).

... MICROSOFT. WHERE WOULD YOU GO? I smile when I see that on the TV that hangs from the ceiling of my cell. It's all so far away now. They go on like before. They'll go on for a long time. They sing, they laugh, they dance and have a great time. Without me. I can't stop coughing. I've gone and got tuberculosis. (The illness is on the increase again, especially within the prison population.)

Everything is transient and everything can be bought, except for Octave. Because I've been bought up already, I've paid for my sins in this hell-hole of a prison. They've allowed me (for a small sum) to watch TV in my cell. People eating. People consuming things. People driving cars. People loving each other. People taking photos of each other. People travelling. People who believe that everything is still possible. People who are happy but don't make the most of it. People who are unhappy but do nothing to remedy it. All the things that people invent so as not to be alone. I'm sure there used to be a slobby cartoon character who said, 'Happy people piss me off.' Happy people (that bloke in glasses, for example, that I can see out of my cell window, at a bus stop with a pretty redhead, squeezing her hand in his in the drizzle), the 'happy few', don't piss me off. They make me cry with rage, jealousy, admiration and frustration.

I imagine Sophie in the moonlight, with a gleam of condensation on her breasts, and Mark stroking the inside of her elbow, in that place which is so soft that it's translucent despite the suntan. The stars are reflected on her moist shoulders. One day, when I die, I'll go and find them, far, very far away, on an island, and I'll piss the sperm out of my dick on to her tongue, her – the mother of my child. And when the sun sets on the horizon, I'll see it. I can already see it on a reproduction of a painting by Gauguin at the end of my piss-stinking cell. I don't know why I cut that particular picture, *La Pirogue*, out of a magazine and hung it above my bed. I'm obsessed with it. I thought I was frightened of death, but I was frightened of life.

They want to separate me from my daughter. They've done everything to stop me seeing your great big eyes. In between bouts of coughing, I have all the time in the world to imagine them. Two great black circles discovering life. Sadists, they're showing that Pampers ad on TV with all those babies sitting in a lecture theatre. They're killing my poor withered lungs. Two sparkling eyes in a pink face. They're stopping me from enjoying it. Her little mouth between her chubby cheeks. Tiny hands clasping my trembling chin. Smelling her milky neck. Burying my nose in her ears. They didn't let me wipe up your poo. They didn't let me dry your tears. They didn't let me welcome you into the world. By killing herself, she assassinated you.

They've deprived me of my daughter, who sleeps curled up in a little ball and scratches her cheeks. She breathes quickly then yawns a little and starts breathing more - slowly, her mini-elbows and miniature knees bent underneath her, my baby with her vampish long eyelashes that curl back, with her rosy red lips and her pale face, a little Lolita whose blood vessels show through the skin at her temples and on her eyelids. They've stopped me from knowing her laughter, the way she squeals when you tickle her nose, her pearly ears like little shells. They've forbidden me from knowing that Chloe was waiting for me at the end of the line. And what if she was what I was looking for when I chased all the girls? That downy neck, those piercing black eyes, those etched eyebrows, those delicate features, I loved them so much in other girls because they were the precursor of my own. I loved cashmere so much only so that I could get used to the feel of your skin. And I went out every night only to get used to your hours.

Hey! And what if it wasn't actually me who was in prison but my lookalike tramp instead, the homeless guy from my street? What if it was him crouched in this shitty cell, while I was out, gone? That's right, you heard me, GONE. I could have changed places with him and he would count himself lucky. He'd have a roof over his head and regular meals, and I'd be free on the other side of the world. Everyone would end up winning. But I'm losing the plot. My lungs have had it.

I've finished my book at £9.99. What a shame, I still keep coming up with new baselines for Yoplite: WHEN YOU WANT TO BE BRIGHT AND BEAUTIFUL . . . FOR A PER-FECT FIGURE AND THE BRAINS TO GO FIGURE . . . HEALTHY LIVING – GOOD THINKING . . . MENS SANA ET CORPORE SANO (nah, think that one's a bit Juvenal).

Because of the bars, the only window in my cell looks like a bar-code.

And on TV they're singing: 'We've got to get outta this place, if it's the last thing we ever doooo.'

And all those murderers on the floor above who are for-ever yelling and moaning and whingeing. For God's sake, they're really getting me down. Should've just stopped to think a bit before knocking people off. They found Charlie bathed in a pool of blood yesterday. He'd opened his veins with a tin of John West sardines. The idiot managed to film himself making this grand gesture with a hidden webcam, and transmitted the scene live on the Net. All that matters is that they haven't caught up with Tamara, I'm glad she managed to get out of it. If it wasn't for that they would've fucked everything up.

As for me, (I'm alone, I've got books and TV, it's OK, even if it does stink of piss and I'm coughing my lungs up), I've Sellotaped Gaugin's *La Pirogue*, a picture dated (1896) on the wall of my VIP cell, as I said. It's in Sergei Chtchoukine's collection and is on display at the Hermitage in Leningrad. I cough in front of this picture all day long: a man, a woman, their child, languishing calmly round their canoe (the *pirogue* of the title) on a Polynesian island.

In one of the last letters of his life Gauguin wrote: 'I am wild and free.'

All I have to do is think that I'm not in prison but delivered of this world. Monks live in cells too.

I look at *La Pirogue*, such an idyllic scene, the couple and their little baby, and in the background Gauguin painted a bright red sunset, it looks like an atomic mushroom cloud, and I swim towards them, I jump into the canoe, I'm going to join them on their island, they're going to love me, I'm swimming towards the beach, past the sunfish and the manta rays that stroke my hands, I'm going to be with them, and we'll all make love together, Tamara with Sophie, Dewler with Browning, I'm going to rise above everything, they've escaped from society, we'll make a new family, we'll fuck as a foursome, and I'll eat Chloe's feet, her tiny feet that fit in the palm of your hand, you'll see, I'm going to join them on their ghostly island, you'd better believe it, yes, it's pretty clear now that I've gone off the rails, and I'm swimming under the sea, breathing in the water, and I feel so good, and Gauguin's sunset really does look like a nuclear explosion.

41

A few months have passed on Ghost Island. They're bored of being dead. They feel that unhappiness is much harder to bear under the sun. They're suffering from good nutrition. They're vegetating amidst all this vegetation. When they're feeling good they go and mix with the other inhabitants: River Phoenix gets Caroline to suck him off while Patrick sodomizes Ayrton Senna; everyone here screws around, fucks arses, sucks cocks, gulps sperm, strokes clitorises, rubs dicks, ejaculates over faces, fingers fannies, whips breasts, pisses over people, frigs and wanks in a state of complete joy and relaxation.

But after a while you get fed up with group sex with seventeen other people. So you perfect your tennis, go deep-sea diving off the atoll, take a spin round the bay, play ping-pong under a giant parasol, play skittles with coconuts wearing just a G-string, compete for bottles of Dom Pérignon, and even, would you believe, only this evening, Caroline herself ironed Patrick's T-shirts. He was quite moved that she called for an ironing board instead of asking for the maids to do it; he would never have guessed he would find such simplicity so touching. They also often relax in insulated chambers which give no form of external stimulus, or on bubbling waterbeds, in between their aroma-therapy massages and their shiatsu sessions.

No alternative to the real world.

Azure, azure, azure, azure, they've had an overdose of azure, they've got paradise indigestion as they lie there on their deck chairs or their *Emmanuelle*-style rattan chairs which scratch your arse, by the pool where Mona, Tania and Lola are frolicking (they're the paid nymphettes whose shaven orifices are discussed and shared out laconically between three beautiful young men with chiselled features). They're growing fat. They've stuffed themselves too much and their bellies hang over their Bermuda shorts which try as best they can to stay up. The bulk always betrays the profiteers. Look at them, the stupid happy bastards, drunk on their own laziness: there's a thick layer of fat over their self-satisfied features. They dance the lambada with perfect impunity. They've run away from the human race, it means less to them than the flowers and the rivers that flow into the sea. They listen to Californian reggae. They're replete with truffles and caviar. As fat as their baby. Caroline mothers her baby, Patrick gardens, the baby babbles. Happiness gives you a hangover.

In 2001, each British household spent an average of £80 a week on food. Coca-Cola sells a million cans an hour round the world. There are 20 million unemployed in Europe.

They want newspapers, television, things happening: all they've got is the balmy torpor of each day just like the one before and the one to follow.

Barbie sells two dolls every second. 2.8 billion inhabitants of this planet live on less than $2 a day. Seventy per cent of *the planet's inhabitants have no telephone and 50 per cent no electricity. The global budget for military expenditure is more than $4,000 billion: that's twice the total national debt of all developing countries.*

Caroline's beginning to find it distasteful raising her daughter in this blasé sect.

'Won't she ever be able to leave? She needs pollution, noise, exhaust fumes!'

Patrick's getting depressed in the bamboo plantation. Even the gentle waves don't lull anyone. The hours are sliding over them. They get drunk on multicoloured cocktails, they have headaches the whole time. The sea air causes migraines. The mirror-like surface of the sea keeps repeating itself. The ocean's going soft in the head.

Bill Gates's personal fortune is equivalent to the GDP of Portugal. Claudia Schiffer's is estimated at more than £20 million. Some 250 million children in the world work for just a few pennies an hour.

Come back, over there, come back! I think the little birds have got migraines . . . Patrick's getting ideas for a poster, a head full of concepts, and they keep coming, they keep coming. He remembers what it was like. FOR THE MEN WHO LIKE MEN WHO LIKE WHORES WHO LIKE COKE WHICH TAKES DOSH.

No alternative to the real world.

They get married, get divorced, get remarried, have children, don't look after them, but bring up other people's children and other people bring theirs up. *Every day the 200 largest fortunes in the world grow by $500 a second.* Dawn is a sunset in auto-reverse. Dusk is a rewound sunrise. In both cases, it's red and it lasts too long. *It is estimated that 25 per cent of all animal species could be wiped off the face of the earth before 2025.* At the end of fairy stories, we always read the same sentence: 'They lived happily ever after and had lots of children.' Full stop. We're never told what happens next: Prince Charming isn't the father of her children, he starts drinking, then leaves the princess for a younger woman, the princess spends fifteen years in therapy, her children get into drugs, the eldest commits suicide, and the youngest becomes a prostitute near King's Cross Station.

Patrick and Caroline spend all day waiting for the evening, and all night waiting for morning. Soon when they make love, they won't be doing it for the pleasure but just for a week's peace. All those crystal-clear inlets, those coral-ringed lagoons, all they actually do is imprison them in blue. Their coral and mangrove cabin is completely surrounded by water. This island is like a haunted castle. Days on end spent plucking petals off daisies: 'I love you, not at all, not much, not really, not all that much, less than yesterday, more than tomorrow.' *The end of the world will come in five billion years, and when the sun explodes, the earth will burn up like a fir cone struck by lightning.* The sunlight filters through the dried palm leaves. The sun is a countdown in yellow light. *General Motors' turnover ($168 billion) is equivalent to the GDP of Denmark.* The moon in the middle of the day, feet swishing in the water, warm waves slapping on wood, the sickly breeze, the smell of the bougainvillaea, clumps of jacaranda. God, it makes you puke, the place smells so strongly of bloody flowers like some shagging air-freshener.

42

But then a day comes when the sky clouds over; and, oh dear, Patrick's letting the current carry him away; and he watches the shore getting smaller and smaller; in the distance on the beach, Caroline's calling him but he can't answer because his mouth's full of salt water; he's floating on his back, carried away on the darker and darker waters, in a deeper and deeper blue; to be carried away; to become a piece of wood; a bottle on the sea with no message in it; and above him there are the birds and below him there are the fish; he comes across sand sharks, sea breams, dolphins; manta rays stroke his hands; and inside Patrick's head this is the end; he's swimming under the sea; he's breathing in the water; he feels so good; 'I bathed in the Poem of the Sea' (Rimbaud); I'm already dead and buried anyway; disperse me between two waters; suddenly it starts raining and the burning droplets sting my face; and the sun's turning red; not slipping between the droplets of crushed glass any more; not conjugating verbs any more; I you he we you they; to become infinitive; like in an instruction booklet or a recipe; to sink; to cross through the mirror; to rest at last; to become one with the elements; rays of ochre and scarlet; nothing existed before the big bang and nothing will survive after the sun explodes; the sky is turning blood red; to drink the tearlike dew drops; so rigorously blue; to fall; to become one with the sea; to become eternity; a minute without breathing, then two, then three; an hour without breathing, then two, then three; in five billion years, the sea will have gone off with the sun; a night without breathing, then two, then three; joining peace once more; 'The stillness of the central sea' (Tennyson); floating on the surface like a water-lily; surfing on an abyss; staying still; lungs full of water; aquatic soul; leaving for good; five billion years earlier: nothing; five billion years later: nothing; man is an accident in the intersidereal vacuum; in order to stop dying you just have to stop living; losing contact; becoming a nuclear submarine hidden in the depths of the ocean; not having any weight any more; swimming between angels and mermaids; swimming through the sky; flying through the sea; everything is consumed; in the beginning was the Word; they say that when you die you see your life flash before you but Patrick saw something completely different – YOU CAN'T FIT QUICKER THAN A KWIK-FIT-FITTER BT ITS GOOD TO TALK ADIDAS FOR EVER SPORT HEARTBEAT THE HEALTHPLAN THAT'S AS INDIVIDUAL AS YOU ARE OUR ULTIMATE FINISH FROM A TO B WE RAC TO IT SIEMENS BE INSPIRED SUCHARD FEED YOUR DESIRE AA THE FOURTH EMERGENCY SERV-ICE SHREWD SHREWDER SCHROEDERS VAUXHALL RAIS-ING THE STANDARD DENTYL PH SURE TO TAKE YOUR BREATH AWAY MFI MAKE IT YOURS FOR LESS ROVER A CLASS OF ITS OWN LANCOME BELIEVE IN BEAUTY THE CAR IN FRONT'S A TOYOTA NORWICH UNION

TOGETHER WE'RE STRONGER ROBINSONS YOU'RE ONLY A GLASS AWAY PEOPLE WHO LIKE FOOD LOVE HELL-MANN'S FORD MONDEO BUILT TO LEAD DEBENHAMS BRITAIN'S FAVOURITE DEPARTMENT STORE ROBERT'S ROCK IT'S THE CHARACTER THAT MAKES THE DIFFER-ENCE SHISEIDO I AM THE SKINCARE RENAULT CLIO SIZE MATTERS ELLESSE THE ART OF SPORT THERE IS LIGHT AND THERE IS OSRAM KARVOL LET THE WHOLE FAMILY GET A QUIET NIGHT HONDA FIRST THE MAN THEN THE MACHINE SURE IT WON'T LET YOU DOWN ROYAL MAIL THINK OF A LETTER MAX FACTOR THE MAKE-UP OF MAKE-UP ARTISTS INTERFLORA SAY IT WITH FLOWERS WITH CLARINS LIFE'S MORE BEAUTIFUL DON'T JUST PAINT IT CROWN IT UNITED COLOURS OF BENETTON SAMSUNG DIGITAL EVERYONE'S INVITED FEDERAL EXPRESS THE WORLD ON TIME GOLF SOME THINGS ARE BEST LEFT ALONE MARKS & SPENCER EXCLUSIVELY FOR EVERYONE YOU CAN DO IT WHEN YOU B & Q IT JAGUAR THE ART OF PERFORMANCE ABBEY NATIONAL BECAUSE LIFE'S COMPLICATED ENOUGH HMV TOP DOG FOR MUSIC ROC WE KEEP OUR PROMISES KA ANY MORE LEATHER AND IT'D MOO QUALITY MOMENTS WITH QUALITY STREET GILLETTE THE BEST A MAN CAN GET ROYAL NAVY THE TEAM WORKS LONGINE ELEGANCE IS AN ATTITUDE NOBODY DOES CHICKEN LIKE KFC GET EXTREME GET RIGHT GUARD SUZUKI RIDE THE WINDS OF CHANGE MAYBELLINE MAYBE SHE'S BORN WITH IT ICELAND ARE WE DOING A DEAL OR ARE WE DOING A DEAL YOU'RE BETTER OFF AT HOMEBASE SKITTLES TASTE THE RAINBOW VISION EXPRESS EXPERTS WITH

VISION TOSHIBA THE POWER TO OPEN PEOPLE'S EYES HP MEALS A REAL MOUTHFUL DIFLUCAN ONE THRUSH NIL VISION FOR EVERYONE IMPERIAL LEATHER RELEASE THE LATHER NEW WALKERS SQUARES THEY'RE WALKERS IN DISGUISE IKEA COME AND SEE US OR WE'LL COME AND SEE YOU VANISH THE SECRET OF STAIN REMOVAL MERCEDES-BENZ FOR WHOEVER YOU ARE MULTIYORK JUST WHAT YOU'VE BEEN LOOKING FOR SO SIMPLE SO SANDERSON MAGNET DESIGNED FOR LIVING BUILT FOR LIFE CIF C THE ONLY DIFFERENCE HOUSE OF FRASER LIBERATE YOUR SENSES HACKETT ESSENTIAL BRITISH KIT APPLE THINK DIFFERENT BANG & OLUFSEN A LIFE LESS ORDINARY VOLVO FOR LIFE LACOSTE BECOME WHAT YOU ARE HEAD OVER HEELS PEUGEOT 106 GTI DO NOT UNDERESTIMATE THE POWER CAMEL ACTIVE ONE LIFE LIVE IT IT'S GOT TO BE GORDON'S AQUASCUTUM NATURAL BORN STYLE ON BUSINESS ON TIME CLAIROL ORGANIC ESSENCE A TOTALLY ORGANIC EXPERIENCE HAVE YOU WOKEN UP TO KELLOGG'S CORNFLAKES EASYJET THE WEB'S FAVOURITE AIRLINE VIRGIN MOBILE NOT JUST A PRETTY FASCIA FALMER SECOND SKIN FRUCTIS FOR HAIR THAT SHINES WITH ALL ITS STRENGTH GIVENCHY BEYOND INFINITY BRITISH AIRWAYS THE WORLD'S FAVOURITE ARILINE PHILIPS LET'S MAKE THE FUTURE BETTER RHONE POULENC WELCOME TO A BETTER WORLD

WELCOME TO A BETTER WORLD.

This book is currently being formatted for computer.

It will soon be the subject of a virtual reality programme available on PC and iMac-compatible CD-Rom. Then you will be able to live it.

The original soundtrack of £9.99 is available on the website www.aprilfirst.com

Tamara was dressed by Stella McCartney for Chloë

Thanks to Manuel Carcassonne, Jean-Paul Enthoven, Gabriel Gaultier, Thierry Gounaud, Michel Houellebecq, Pamela Le Moult, Pascal Manry, Vincent Ravalec, Stéphane Richard, Delphine Vallette.

This book is their fault too.

Lines from 'Where do I Begin' © Francis Lai and Carl Sigman, quoted by permission of Memory Lane Music.

Extract from *Brave New World* by Aldous Huxley, published by Chatto & Windus. Reprinted by permission of The Random House Group Ltd and The Aldous Huxley Literary Estate.

Extract from *Fear and Loathing in Las Vegas* by Hunter S. Thompson, published by Flamingo, an imprint of HarperCollins Publishers Ltd.

Every effort has been made to trace the copyright holders but if any have been inadvertently overlooked the publishers will be pleased to make the necessary arrangement at the first opportunity.

picador.com

blog
videos
interviews
extracts

Lightning Source UK Ltd.
Milton Keynes UK
UKHW041215250621
386146UK00004B/737

9 781447 272229